My thank you is to my Father-in-Law, Thomas, for proof reading and providing the corrections to my spelling and grammar errors.

This is a work of fiction and any similarities to any person is coincidental, places mentioned may or may not exist or be as described as I have used a fair bit of dramatic licence when writing. If you enjoy this book please leave me a (good) review on Amazon. To keep up with future books please follow me on Instagram or Facebook.

Prologue

The fresh, undisturbed, light layer of snow crunched under foot as the group of eight people made their way slowly down the hill that was close to their target. Rifles up and ready, scanning for any possible threats. They hadn't seen anyone in the time that had taken to walk from the house where they had taken shelter the night before and where they were now. A pandemic had killed off the majority of the world's population nine months before. A group of twenty survivors had beaten off an attack by another group looking for slaves before taking over a village nestled in a valley. The group of twenty had grown to over eighty, living in close proximity to each other and working to

Instagram danielpbaldockauthor

Facebook Daniel P Baldock Author

EXTINCTION

SURVIVING THE NEW NORMAL

By Daniel P Baldock

Cover Photography by Daniel P Baldock

From the Author

As a self-published author your support means a lot. I'll start with a thank you to you, the reader, for buying this book. The first book in this series was my way of keeping busy during the Covid-19 pandemic whilst I was furloughed. My second book was a way of passing the time whilst my now wife planned most of our wedding day and this book has been a chance to expand on what I have learnt whilst writing my first two books and to re-visit my first published characters.

My next thank you is to my darling wife, Grace, for her support and encouragement whilst I wrote this book. Our days out together helped inspire me to write about these places in my book. Without her this book would have taken a lot longer or not happened at all.

keep the village fed. This group of eight were the scouting party. The lead man stopped and knelt down, his breath coming out as steam and swirling around in the light of the full moon. He pulled a map from his jacket and looked at it. A part of him wished his phone still worked so he could double check his navigation but the pandemic had turned phones into paper weights. He stood up again and moved forward, the rest followed him. The road they were on climbed slightly and turned right, they followed it and they found the junction they were looking for. The lead man headed down the small hill and looked around. He saw the building which he was looking for. He gathered the group and looked at each of them.

"Chris, Jamal, round the back. James, Peter, cover the front. Elliot, stay here. Leo, Marcus, with me.

We are going to the front and to find a way in." He briefed.

"Jake, is that a good idea?" A tall man with greying hair asked.

"Best I've got." Jake replied. He put a fist out and each one of them bumped it with their own.

Jake watched as everyone else moved off. He started his walk to the front of the building. There was no sign of anyone being around, the snow was smooth, no sign of footprints. He reached the stairs to the entrance and paused. Listening for anything that was out of place. Leo and Marcus were behind. Jake started climbing the stairs. Marcus and Leo covered the windows at the entrance. Jake reached the switchback on the staircase and turned. He put his foot on the next step and transferred his weight to it. He took the next step and slipped, landing with a thud against the stairs. He swore and got up.

"Enjoy the trip?" Leo joked quietly but loud enough for Jake to hear.

Jake responded with his middle finger and climbed the stairs. He tried the door. It was locked. He removed a small pouch from his jacket and took out the contents. He picked the lock in under a minute and let himself in. Marcus and Leo followed him. They cleared the building as best they could in the dark before calling the others in. Jake locked the door again and then led them deeper into the building. They all dropped their rucksacks and sat down in office chairs around the room where they had stopped. It was almost pitch black in the room.

"We set up in here for tonight. Tomorrow, we take stock of everything in here and then we prepare to get everything moved back to the village." Jake ordered.

"I'll take first watch." Chris offered.

Nobody objected and they all spread out to find somewhere to put out a sleeping bag. Jake found a corner and unrolled his sleeping bag. He then pulled out a small stuffed tiger and put it next to him. He climbed into the sleeping bag and was asleep two minutes later.

#

Chapter 1

Four Months Before

Jake reached the summit of the hill first. His mind telling him to drop low and avoid standing out, he ignored it and looked around, the deserted urban sprawl of a now almost deserted Eastbourne behind him, the rolling hills of the South Downs in front of him. It was a week since he had led the defence of the campsite where the group of survivors he was with had taken shelter as well as the liberation of another group. The week had been busy. Most of the group of sixty had been out loading up lorries and vans with as much food, clothes, building supplies and spare fuel as possible. Jake had led a small group to a village that was built either side of a river which cut through the south downs a few miles outside of Eastbourne. It was a few miles inland, just far enough off main roads that it wasn't likely to be found easily but close enough that it wouldn't take too long to get to. They had cleared the village by stealth, picking locks and searching every house but finding no survivors. It had taken two days to remove all the dead bodies from the houses and bury them in a mass grave. Jake had left four people in the village to act as security, not that they expected any problems. He had headed back with Chris, the man who had become his closest friend since the pandemic, and, when he really thought about it, his closest friend ever. They had explained everything to the rest of the survivors and agreed that they would move as soon as they had taken everything they could and loaded it all into the lorries which were running low on fuel. He had agreed to head back to the village and be ready to meet the group when they arrived in two days. Chris was going to lead the survivors to the village. Jake looked back at the three people behind him. Will, his friend from before the pandemic, and someone he had served with in the Army, was at the front. He was a farmer and was going ahead to start looking at setting up a farm on the outskirts of the village. Jenny, a teenage girl, who had been rescued by Jake just before the battle against the other group, followed Will, carrying a rucksack weighing about half her weight but not complaining. Bringing up the rear was Rob, a newcomer to the group, rescued from the other survivors. He had volunteered to come along. He had been a mechanic before the pandemic. Jake watched him move, bringing up the rear. They all reached the summit of the hill and sat on the grass verge at the side of the road.

"Remind me, why aren't we taking a car?" Rob panted.

"Conserving all the fuel for the move, plus it's good exercise." Will answered.

"We will run out of fuel soon, so it makes sense to get the practice in." Jake added.

After resting for ten minutes, they got up and followed the road leading from Eastbourne towards East Dean. They followed it into the dip and then pushed themselves to climb the hill the other side. They reached the top and all sat down. Jake wiped the sweat away from his eyes.

"Bloody hell, at least it's all down hill from here." He said breathing heavily.

"We definitely need to find an alternative to cars." Jenny added.

"Add it to the long list of things we have to do." Rob huffed.

It took another four hours of walking before they reached the village. Jake dropped his rucksack at the entrance to the house in the middle of the village. The others did the same before sitting down in the shade and taking a drink from their water bottles.

"Take an hour, select somewhere to move into and then meet back here and we will start assigning uses for buildings." Jake ordered.

Will, Jenny and Rob got up and walked off. Jake grabbed his rucksack and headed north through the village. He had pretty much decided on the house he wanted. It was near the northern entrance to the village, a cottage straight out of a postcard, with a low brick wall and flowers in the front garden which he could cut back and tame. He had unlocked the door on his first visit to

the village. He went in and put his rucksack down. He

looked around and then headed back to the meeting point.

#

Chapter 2

The holiday park seemed small now that it was home for four times as many as it had a week before. Laura watched her two children playing. The last week had been the most relaxed she had felt for a long time. Before the pandemic, it was a struggle to keep a roof over their heads and food on the table. During the pandemic it had been a fight for survival, snatching sleep but never fully relaxing. Since meeting the group of survivors and especially Jake she had been able to let her guard down. Unburdened by money issues and having other people to keep her and her children safe, she felt that life seemed to be better. A smile crossed her face. The move was rapidly approaching. Twenty lorries of various sizes and styles had been liberated and were being loaded with as much as possible: clothing, food, building materials, toys, medicine and anything else that people felt would be important and could find a space for. She had been excused from loading so that she could keep Alex and Chloe occupied. A wet nose nudged her hand. Timber was a dog rescued by Jake not long after Laura and Jake had met. Timber was almost constantly by her side now. She rubbed his head. The madness was nothing compared to what it had been. Laura yawned, the pace of the last week catching up with her. Everyone was due to leave as soon as the lorries were loaded. She watched the leader of the group give out directions and helped move items from a store cupboard to the rear of one of the lorries. It wasn't going to be much longer before they left in a convoy which would take them towards the next part of their lives. Alex and Chloe both ran over to her and hugged a leg each.

"Hey, have you finished packing?" Laura asked them both.

"Yes!" they answered together.

"Good."

"Will I have my own room at the new place?" Chloe asked.

"I should hope so." Laura grinned, "We may even be able to paint it."

Laura noticed the leader stop moving. A lot of the activity had stopped at the same time.

"All of the lorries are packed. We leave in one hour." He shouted.

Laura turned to the kids and smiled again.

"Grab your bags, we are off."

"Yay!" Alex and Chloe cheered

#

Chapter 3

The convoy rolled past Jake and into the village. The lorries headed to their assigned drop off points. The cars and vans were parked in the car park in the middle of the village and the roads around it. Jake hugged, shook hands with and greeted virtually everyone as they arrived. He scanned the faces for Laura, Alex and Chloe. He couldn't see them. Thirty minutes after the last vehicle arrived, everybody gathered outside the church.

"Welcome everyone," Jake started, "There's lots to do and not that many of us to do it. Justin will come up with the grand plan and brief everyone on it in due course."

"Good luck!" Someone from the back shouted.

"We need to get the lorries unloaded and two guard posts set up, one each end of the village. We will have to make scout parties and community rules." Jake carried on. "First of all though, there is a small matter of housing. Keys are in doors. Some doors have been labelled for important people, those who need to be in the middle of the village or for everyone to know where they live. Find a house, sort out your belongings and prepare to be busy. Meet back here in two hours."

"Nice one Jake!" Someone else shouted.

Jake watched the crowd disperse. An older man came over and shook his hand.

"Justin, hope you are ready for this?" Jake grinned.

"Nope, there is a lot to do, we need to get a team of leaders together to run this place."

"We'll get there, one issue at a time."

"I hope so, see you in a bit."

Jake stood by himself, his mind running through everything which needed to happen, food store, dining area, clothing stores, equipment stores, farm set-up, school provision, medical, firefighting and fire lighting. Justin would be busy arranging it all. Jake would help where he could, leading search parties and keeping people safe.

"Hey, you found us a house yet?" Laura asked from behind him.

Jake turned and saw Laura, Alex and Chloe standing in a group. He walked over and hugged Laura, kissing her on the forehead and then hugging Alex and Chloe as well.

"Yes, yes I have." Jake smiled.

"Let's go then," Laura prompted.

#

Chapter 4

Laura had stayed back and out of sight to give

Jake his moment, He had made the move happen, he had

found the village and he had earned the right to stand in

front of the group. He held her hand and they walked

together with Alex, Chloe and Timber in front of them.

Jake gave them all directions. They rounded a corner and

before Jake could say anything Laura knew it was the

one he had chosen. It was straight out of a postcard, the

garden was a bit overgrown but it had a low wall

separating it from the road, with white walls and a black

front door.

"What do you think?" Jake asked "Look like

home?"

"Yes, you've made the right choice." She smiled, "It's perfect."

"You've not seen inside yet."

Jake opened the front door; Alex and Chloe ran in and started looking around. Laura did the same. The front door opened into a narrow hallway with stairs on the left side. The lounge was on the right, the furniture was a bit old fashioned but it was a nice size and had a dining table and chairs. The walls were a light yellow and there were some paintings on the wall as decoration. Laura walked round into the kitchen, which was a good size, more modern than the lounge and with a utility room at the far end.

"Yay, we can have our own rooms!" Alex and Chloe cheered at the same time.

Laura followed the sound of their voices and found them upstairs, Alex in one room, Chloe in another and a third bedroom that nobody was in. She turned and hugged Jake who had followed her round the house.

"Thank you, it's perfect." She said fighting back tears of joy.

Jake wrapped her in a hug. They stood together whilst Alex and Chloe excitedly explored the house. Jake eventually let go.

"I'm glad you like it." He said "I can't wait to live here with you."

Laura looked around again, amazed by how life had changed so much in such a short space of time, from being a single mum trying to raise two kids, then the virus, trying to survive in the world after the pandemic and then meeting Jake, the group and surviving that encounter. Now she had a partner, a house and safety.

Jake explained he had work to do and left them to

explore the house. Alex and Chloe had decided on their

rooms and were now wanting to get their possessions.

Laura told them to wait and then started exploring the

house in more detail.

#

Chapter 5

Jake yawned. Unloading had taken three times as long as the loading and with different locations around the village for different things it had been a challenge to make sure everything was in the right place. Justin had asked for several people to meet in the village hall and Jake had been one of the lucky few. He looked at the group whilst they waited for Justin. Chris sat next to Jake, Will on the other side of Jake. Jessie, an older woman who used to run a café that Jake had grown very fond of in the time they had known each other, was sitting on the other side of Chris. Another older woman, Eileen, was next to Jessie; Eileen had been a doctor before the virus. On the other side of Will was Rob. Across the room and standing up was another group of four, Henry, a tall broad man who had once been a builder, Peter, a short slim man who had only recently joined the group and whom Jake didn't know much about, Clara, a tall woman who had been an engineer, and Lionel, a very plain looking man who was of average height and build, a plumber before the virus. Justin walked in with Jenny next to him.

"Right, thanks for coming, I have a huge list of things to get through and you are my chosen council, Heads of Departments, if you prefer." He started. "Jenny is going to be my secretary."

"Right ok." Chris replied a bit stunned.

"You all have an area of expertise that we need. Chris, you are education, you are in charge of the school; if and when the community needs education and kids need schooling, you will lead it. Will, you are farming, anyone you want to help you do it will be assigned to it. It will be our main source of food for years to come. Rob, you are maintenance of machinery and vehicles. Jessie, I'd like you to run the dining hall and community hub. As we don't have power or gas for every house I want to limit it to one central place. Jake, dual role, safety here and exploring the area, finding other survivors, setting up links with them."

"OK." Jake nodded.

"Eileen, can you be our doctor? We are going to need someone to keep us all healthy. Henry, Peter, Clara and Lionel: our maintenance and development team. Between you I'd like to know if there is a way of getting power, heating and fresh water for the village."

"We may be able to knock something together." Henry replied.

"Thank you. Unless anyone objects we should meet daily for the next week or so to discuss progress." Justin finished. "Today's been hard. Let's get some rest and start again tomorrow."

Jake left the meeting with his head spinning. How to keep the village safe and secure and how to explore and where to explore? He reached the house and was greeted by an excited Timber.

#

Chapter 6

Laura woke up to find the bed empty. Her first thought was to check on Alex and Chloe. As she got out of the bed and her feet landed on the soft carpet, she remembered where she was. She stood up, grabbed a soft pink dressing gown from a hook on the back of the bedroom door and wrapped it around her. She checked both rooms. Alex was fast asleep, cuddling a stuffed tiger that Jake had found for him. Chloe was awake and playing with a stuffed Labrador, again a gift from Jake. Chloe smiled and said hello before Laura closed the door and went downstairs. Jake was on the sofa, hunched over a map laid out on the coffee table. She walked round and gave him a kiss on the top of his head. He looked up and grinned.

"Looks fun," she joked. "Anything I can help with?"

"Just looking at maps and planning for the future." Jake shrugged,

"Don't stress about it, there's a lot of people here to help."

"Thanks."

A knock at the door distracted both of them. Jake stood up and went to answer it, Laura followed him. Jake opened the door to find an out-of-breath Jenny panting.

"It's Justin, he's collapsed, they sent me to get you. They think it may be a stroke."

"Where is he?"

"The church."

Laura watched as Jake ran off, Jenny following. She closed the door and tried to process what had just been said. She took a deep breath and closed the door. She went back upstairs and changed into leggings and a hoodie. Alex had woken up and walked out onto the landing.

"I'm hungry, can we have breakfast?" he asked.

"Yes, let's go get breakfast." She smiled "Get dressed and we will get breakfast."

"Yay." Alex cheered.

Ten minutes later Laura led Chloe and Alex to the restaurant which was going to be the community dining area. By the time they arrived there was a buzz around the place, people talking about Justin and the stroke. She found a table and sat Alex and Chloe down before going to get a bowl of fruit salad for each of them. They had looted every possible can of food from the supermarkets during the week of planning for the move.

She set the bowls down just as Jake walked in looking shocked.

#

Chapter 7

Jake arrived at the church to find a small group of people around Justin. Eileen was crouched over him. She looked up as Jake arrived and shook her head. Jake froze, stunned. He looked at the group, everyone looking on, nobody sure what to say and do, tears on some faces.

"What happened?" Jake eventually managed to ask.

"Rob found him in here, slumped in the pew. He's gone, it looks to me like a stroke." Eileen answered. "What do we do now?"

"We need to appoint a new leader, do we tell everyone?" Jenny asked.

"Jake, you are in charge, you are the best person for it." Rob said.

"He's right, Jake, you need to take Justin's place," Jenny seconded.

"Agreed," Everyone else nodded.

"It's what Justin would have wanted." Rob finished.

"I don't know." Jake started.

"We do. You know that if it went to a vote you'd be voted in anyway." Jenny replied.

"Ok, I guess. I'll go and break the news to everyone now." Jake shrugged reluctantly.

He looked down at Justin, who looked peaceful, smaller than when he had been alive. His face was paler. Jake tried to process what had happened. Justin had once said he would lead the group to safety, perhaps he had and now he had achieved his aim he had given up. It hit Jake like a hammer blow to the chest. He was now responsible for everyone, keeping them all safe, ensuring they could live. He turned and left the church. He walked to the restaurant where everyone would be eating breakfast. He entered and saw Laura and the kids. Everyone else turned to look at him.

"I have some news. You may have heard a rumour about Justin, which sadly I can confirm is true. He was found this morning in the church, unresponsive. Despite Eileen's best efforts he has passed away." Jake said bluntly. "It will be put to a vote for who takes over from him, Until that happens I have agreed to fill his shoes."

"You get my vote!" Jessie shouted from the back of the room.

Most of the room agreed. Laura hugged him, squeezing harder than normal. Jake sat down with Laura,

Alex and Chloe. He kept quiet while they ate. People came past and offered any help they could give as they left. Jake felt the pressure. He had been fine with the idea of security and exploring but now he had to be responsible for everything and everyone.

After breakfast he walked to Justin's house and let himself in. He felt weird standing in the hallway. Justin had barely had time to look round but even so he was inside someone else's house. He was hoping to find something to help him, notes Justin might have made with plans on or ideas. Jake didn't know where to start. He found nothing, no notes, no plans.

#

Chapter 8

Laura watched as Alex and Chloe ran ahead,

exploring the village. They had already found a play

park not far from the house. It was still a hive of activity,

people clearing houses and shops, stacking supplies or

doing their own exploring. She caught sight of Jake a

couple of times but he was deep in conversation with

someone or too far-away for her to catch his attention.

She couldn't imagine what was going on in his head, the

responsibility that had been pushed on to him. As Alex

and Chloe passed the restaurant Jessie came out and saw

them.

"Hello, how are you?" Jessie asked Laura.

"I'm good, the village is nice." Laura smiled,

"You?"

"It is, busy, having to clean all the plates and bowls by hand is a nightmare."

"I bet, we can help if you want?" Laura offered.

"How about Alex and Chloe help and you go and see if Jake needs your help?" Jessie countered, "The poor boy is going to need it."

"I couldn't ask you do to that."

"You didn't, I offered."

Laura thought about it and then took Jessie up on the offer. She told Alex and Chloe to behave and then went to find Jake. She found him in the community centre. Jake was deep in conversation with Jenny. Laura walked over and joined them.

"I'm not an expert, I don't know what we need to do." Jake said

"Justin didn't leave any notes. I don't know what to suggest."

"Make a planning group, use the people around you?" Laura offered.

Twenty minutes later Jake had followed Laura's suggestion. He had gathered the group from last night and was standing in front of a white board.

"I'm going to be honest, I am out of my depth, I have no idea what Justin had planned." Jake started.

"Not sure any of us do." Will joked, trying to lighten the mood.

"What are the essentials for survival? Food, water, shelter." Chris began, "We have water. Everyone is working to install water collectors all over the village. We have the river as well. Food, we have stockpiles of most things and the farm is being assessed and Will is going to expand it. Shelter, everyone has that. We have the basics, the rest is luxury."

"We have an idea for making life better. We could set up solar panels and batteries to store electricity all over the village, We could even look at rigging the village into its own network. We would need a lot of equipment we don't currently have but we think it can be done." Henry stood up. "It isn't perfect but it means we can use radios to communicate, have light and use electric cookers."

"I like it." Laura said, "What about heating and running water?"

"Heating could be electric heaters. Running water is much more difficult."

"Ok. Get me a list of everything you need and we will find it." Jake stated

"I have an idea for vehicles; if we can get electricity, we can power electric vehicles. We may also need larger load-carrying vehicles when fuel for the lorries runs out." Rob explained. "I'll make something up as a prototype."

"Who leads the search teams?" Jenny asked. "Jake? He should stay here in case he is needed. The search teams could be away for extended periods of time."

"Is there anyone else?" Laura asked.

"Not really." Chris shrugged.

"I have an idea, I'll lead the search team. Laura and Jenny you will run things here in my absence." Jake suggested

"Are you sure?" Jenny asked.

"Yes," Jake replied, sounding more certain.

The planning carried on for another three hours,
lists were compiled, ideas shared and roles delegated.

#

Chapter 9

Everyone had gathered in the community centre. Jake was standing on the stage, the planning group behind him. He took a deep breath and tried to calm himself.

"Right, we have a plan. For this to work we need everyone to come together." He started, "Will is going to run the farm and be in charge of food production. He needs lots of people to work alongside him. We also need some people to join the scout team, looking for resources and helping to build links with other survivors. You can do both, if you wish to."

"Will there be other jobs as well?" someone from the back asked.

"Yes as time goes on. For now, Will needs as many people as he can to get the farm going and finish setting up the village. If you want to be involved with the farm please speak to Will, If you want to join the scouting team speak to me." Jake continued, "Those up here with me are going to be overseeing projects and may approach you to help them with things."

"What about water? Toilets?" the same person asked.

"We will install water collectors on the outside of every occupied house and at various other buildings. We will build composting toilets. This is not going to be easy. It will be hard but together we will get through this." Laura answered. "Chris will be starting a school, Jessie will be continuing with the food."

Jake closed the meeting and chatted to fifteen people who wanted to join the scouting team, He saw Will with at least double that number. It was dark by the time he walked home. The stars were bright and clear. Jake walked through the door and was greeted by Laura. She kissed him and then sat with him on the sofa.

"We bury Justin in the morning and then we go back to making the village work for us." Jake sighed.

"No time to mourn at the moment. We will one day." Laura replied.

"Thank you for everything," Jake said. "I couldn't do this without you."

"I'll remind you of that every chance I get." Laura joked.

#

Chapter 10

Laura was impressed at how quickly things had come together. Justin's funeral had been simple and everyone had been able to pay their respects. They had all then gone to work, water butts had been fitted to dozens of buildings, stockpiles of equipment made and lists made of everything they had in the stockpiles. She walked down the main road, looking at the changes taking place in front of her. A group of women were walking down one of the side roads carrying bags which were full to the top. They turned and went into the restaurant. Laura changed direction and followed them in.

"We have been going through all the empty houses and asked everyone to go through their own and collect all the food we can get." One of them said to Jessie.

"Oh wow, thank you." Jessie exclaimed

"Where would you like it?" another asked.

"Upstairs, all the food we have brought with us is up there." Jessie pointed

"Can I help?" Laura offered.

"It's ok, we've got it." The first woman said before they walked off and up the stairs.

Laura and Jessie exchanged a look and waited until the women were upstairs before talking.

"That's a lot of food. Are you getting help with cooking?" Laura asked.

"I am, there's a small team that have offered to help." Jessie grinned "Where are the kids?"

"School, Chris has started already."

"Wow, he isn't hanging around."

"Nope. There are a couple of other children in there as well."

"Let's hope the school grows and he gets more students."

"Well, Jake is training up his team at the moment so it may not be too much longer."

"When is his first scouting trip?"

"As soon as they are ready. They are going to head towards Brighton and see what it is like that way."

They chatted for another five minutes before Laura made her excuse to leave and carried on her tour of the village. She stopped on one of the bridges and watched the river flowing past. A memory ran through her mind: she was with her parents, visiting an old village somewhere, she couldn't remember where; there had been a mill and the mill was powered by a wheel in the river which the water turned. She came back to the present and ran off towards the community centre.

#

Chapter 11

Jake was second in the line, behind a young lad with an Irish accent called Connor, Jake barely knew him but he had shown the most potential in the scout party. They had set off at first light. Less than twenty-four hours since Justin's funeral and they were off. The eight of them were all armed, ready for anything. They had three days of food with them. Each of them carrying a sleeping bag and four bottles of water . The road was fairly flat from the village towards the coast. Connor reached a junction and looked at the sign on top of a white post: Left or right. Connor turned right and they headed along another road, bushes lining the sides and blocking access to the fields. Jake watched Connor, whom he had come across from the group against which

Jake's group had been fighting. Connor hadn't been one of the bad apples. Barely nineteen, he had been one of those forced to farm and provide food for the few who had let power go to their heads. Jake could see the caution that Connor had, not quite certain in what he was doing but doing it anyway. They reached the outskirts of Seaford before stopping. They took five minutes before setting off again. There were no signs of human life anywhere, but plenty of birds, cats and a couple of rabbits. They reached the middle of town and looked in the windows of the shops, making notes of ones that contained anything useful. Jake took over from Connor for the next leg. They walked into Newhaven without seeing a single person. They checked the industrial estates for supplies, finding more than they had imagined.

"We need to get the vehicles down here. We will need all of them to get this stuff back. We can't afford to waste time." Jake said.

"Send a runner back to get them?" Connor suggested.

"Don't be daft, lad." An older man scoffed, "We can't send just one person."

"Peter is right. Connor, Leo, Marcus and Peter, you will head back now, tell them what we have and that every vehicle needs to come. I'll stay here with Jamal, James and Hugo."

"Ok, we'll be back soon," Connor said, turning to leave.

Jake watched them go, part of him wanting to go with them, and lead from the front. He took a deep breath, wished them luck, then pulled out the map and

started looking at areas to move on to.

#

Chapter 12

The quickest route was also the hardest route. Connor had decided against going straight up and over the hills back to the village. They headed north towards the A27. They reached it and quickened the pace. They had stopped looking for danger or other people. Connor led the way, rifle in hand. He found it odd to be walking down the middle of a road which once would have been impossible to walk along safely. They crossed a bridge and came to a roundabout where they could take either north to Lewes or east towards their destination. Connor was halfway across the roundabout when he heard a shout. He turned and saw three men, big broad men holding shotguns.

"Hi," Connor shouted back

"Can we help you?" the tallest one asked, walking towards Connor.

"I'm ok," Connor paused, something stopped him saying where he was heading.

Peter, Leo and Marcus were all out of sight; they had frozen when they heard the shout. Connor could see them out of the corner of his eye.

"There's a tax for passing through our land," the tallest said.

"Oh, I didn't realise this was anyone's land." Connor replied calmly,

"Give us your stuff." The man demanded.

Connor flicked the safety catch of his rifle to the fire position. A small movement the man approaching him didn't notice.

"Now." Another man growled.

Connor took half a step back, his mind screaming for action, telling him it was not going to end well. The tallest man started to raise his shotgun. Connor raised his rifle and fired in one movement. The round caught the man in the upper chest, spinning him, the man's finger tightened on the trigger of the shotgun and fired a round. There was a whistle as the pellets flew past Connor's head. Connor ducked and fired again, the round punching through the man's throat, blood spraying into the air. The other two men opened fire as Peter, Leo and Marcus came into view, their rifles firing in unison, cutting down the two men who didn't get a chance to fire again. Peter applied his safety catch and turned to look at Connor. Peter froze. Connor was clutching his neck, blood spurting out between his fingers. Connor dropped to his knees as Peter ran towards him.

"Stay with me, don't you dare die!" Peter shouted, knowing it was futile.

"Shit!" Leo screamed as he saw what was happening.

Peter lowered Connor to the ground and tried to apply pressure to the wound. He could hear Connor's breathing getting more laboured. He looked into Connor's eyes and saw the life drain out of them.

"Fuck, fucking arseholes!" He screamed.

Marcus stood stunned, rifle by his side. Leo ran to the nearest dead man and started kicking the body.

"Enough!" Peter shouted after a minute. "Grab their weapons. Move them out of the way and find something to carry Connor."

#

Chapter 13

Laura attached the down pipe to the water butt and stepped back. It was the eighth that she had helped fit that day. She had kissed Jake goodbye and then after breakfast dropped Alex and Chloe at school. The morning had been a blur of activity. She had spoken to Rob and Henry about her idea of a water mill. They had given it some thought and were going to do some thinking. She had then joined in with fitting water butts to buildings. She turned and saw Peter walking into the village, head down looking upset. Leo and Marcus were behind him carrying a loaded sheet between them. She gasped and then ran to them.

"Who?" She asked barely able to get the word out.

"Connor." Peter replied subdued.

"How."

"Bandits."

"The others?"

"Newhaven."

Laura wanted to ask more, but Leo and Marcus passed her and she saw Connor's lifeless body. Apart from his damaged throat and the dried blood, he looked asleep.

"We need to get the vehicles to Newhaven with as many people as possible to gather the supplies that we found." Peter said, "Leo, Marcus, get him to the graveyard and start digging the hole."

Laura looked around, suddenly feeling exposed. Like most people she had stopped carrying her rifle when they had taken over the village, feeling safe and secure. Now she wished the rifle wasn't at home. Peter walked off and she ran home, She grabbed the rifle from the cupboard where it had been left in since she had felt safe and thought it was no longer needed, slung it over her shoulder and went back outside. By the time she reached the town centre the first vehicles were leaving. A few people stood watching them go,

"From now on, everyone carries a rifle at all times." Laura told them, "Spread the word."

Laura walked to the graveyard and found Leo and Marcus digging a hole. She knelt down by Connor's body. A tear ran down her cheek. She hadn't known him well but he had seemed full of hope for the future.

"What happened?" She asked

"It happened as we approached a roundabout outside of Lewes. He was out in front, someone shouted at him, he turned and said hello. They asked what he was doing, he said walking and they said that it was their land and there was a tax for passing through it." Marcus tried to explain. "We didn't see them. Connor was ahead of us. I guess they thought he was an easy target."

"Connor took one down and they opened fire as we came into view. One of their shotgun rounds must have caught him, a freak shot. We took them down. They hadn't got much with them, just the shotguns they used, some basic food and bottles of water. Nobody rushed to their aid. We grabbed their shotguns, took their stuff and moved their bodies away from the road." Leo continued to explain.

"Five minutes either way, we don't encounter them, Connor lives." Marcus said

"We need to act as if we are in danger at all times." Laura stated boldly.

\#

Chapter 14

Jake watched as the convoy pulled in. Peter climbed out of the first lorry and Jake saw the dried blood straight away as well as the look on Peter's face. He felt a lump form in his throat. He knew something bad had happened.

"Everything we can fit in to the lorries goes in," Peter shouted. "We left two at the supermarkets to empty them."

The group that had travelled with the convoy spread out and started gathering everything they could. Building materials, equipment and parts were all stacked carefully to maximise the space available.

"What happened?" Jake asked as Peter approached him.

"Bandits, at least I think they were." Peter started. "We ran into them near Lewes, Connor was in front, they saw him, there was a brief exchange of words and Connor opened fire. Took one down, there were two more. An unlucky shot hit him in the neck. Leo, Marcus and myself took them down. Connor bled out there, we couldn't stop it."

"Damn it!" Jake swore, anger rising inside him.

"Nobody could have predicted it."

"I should have been there."

Jake and Peter stared at each other. Peter knew that anything he said would fall on deaf ears. He walked off and started to load stores onto one of the lorries. Jake needed time alone, to process in his mind what he had just heard. He had lost people close to him before. Friends had died on his tours with the army. This felt different, was this was on him? He had sent Connor back, had sent him to his death. Was it down to a lack of training? Jake's mind raced with questions. He shook his head, trying to clear the voice asking the questions. A second voice came in and told him to get on with his job. Jake listened to it, went back and joined in the loading of the lorries. When everything they could fit in had been loaded, they climbed back into the vehicles. Jake and the scout party decided to head back as well. It didn't feel right to carry on searching in the wake of the news that Connor had been killed.

#

Chapter 15

Laura stood in the dining hall. Alex and Chloe had already eaten and one of the older women in the group, Helen, had agreed to babysit them whilst Laura was in a meeting. Everyone was seated and enjoying the tinned meat and veg which Jessie and her team had prepared. She looked around at them. Over half now had weapons with them. Jake's stockpile which he had looted from the armoury of his base in the aftermath of the pandemic was now being used.

"You must be careful. You need to have your weapon with you at all times." She shouted. "What happened to Connor is a tragedy; his death should be a reminder that we aren't safe. We don't know who else is out there."

"Anyone who wants weapon training can see Jamal after dinner. He will arrange it." Will added.

After eating, people filed out, some speaking to Jamal. Laura watched. Jamal had agreed to train people when he heard what had happened to Connor. The last person left the room and Laura, Will and Jamal stood in the empty room. Jessie came through from the kitchen.

"We should head to the community centre." Jessie said with a sigh.

"I don't know if I can face the meeting." Laura said. "This is meant to be our safe haven, the meeting is going to change that."

"It's a new world now, what we thought of as safe is gone, the new normal is not normal yet." Will shrugged.

They walked to the community centre in a group, the last of the planning group to arrive. Jake was already at the front, a map of the village on the whiteboard. Laura could see the tension in his body.

"I'm sorry, I let you all down. I didn't think of security." Jake apologised.

"It isn't your fault." Chris replied. "We all relaxed."

"We have already got plans." Will explained looking at Jake. "Jamal is going to train everyone who wants it on weapons. Everyone has been told they need to carry their rifle,"

"Oh, OK." Jake responded. "I should have told everyone this stuff, I should have arranged it."

"This is new to all of us. Stop beating yourself up. Nobody blames you." Will snapped back. "If Connor had taken a different route, stopped to drink, piss, tie a boot lace, walked slower or faster or do any number of other things he would still be alive."

"Exactly, it was bad luck and bad timing, nothing can plan for that." Peter said

"I still want to set up two guard points, one each end of the village on the road. Take it in turns to man them." Jake said firmly, marking them on the map.

"Fine. Add it to the growing list of shit to do. We are far enough off main routes that anyone out there won't stumble on to us. They would have to be looking and not every survivor we come across will be dangerous." Chris argued. "Stop the pity party and let's get stuff done."

Laura watched the encounter, waiting for an opportunity to jump in. She wanted to take Jake to one side and check on him. He was different, less sure of himself. She stood up and turned to face the group.

"Jake, you can take the scouting party and set up the guard posts. For the next month we don't go out, we stay in and around the village. Settle in. In a month we start local and spread out slowly." Laura began laying out her plan. "We need to get settled here before we look any further. Should anyone stumble across us then great, we can chat, see what they are doing, offer them to join us or visit us again but we focus on here and focus on us."

She had been thinking about it since helping bury Connor. The village was in need of a lot of work, lots of little jobs. She didn't know where to start but she knew that going out and scouting was not the right idea until they had really established a solid foundation. She could see people processing the idea.

"A month works. By then we will have the farm up and running." Will agreed.

"It's a solid plan." Elaine nodded.

Laura took the whiteboard pen from Jake and started writing lists of jobs on the board. She stepped back and looked at what she had written.

"We are the team that will deliver this. Meet back here daily after evening meal to discuss progress." Laura stated. "Now I need to get home. Alex and Chloe are probably driving Helen crazy by now."

The group dispersed. Jake waited for Laura. He hugged her, then kissed her.

"I'm sorry." He said as tears started to flow.

"Don't be, none of this is your fault." She comforted him,

"I'm so proud of you for what you just did."

"Behind every great man, is a woman telling him what to do." She laughed.

Jake laughed back, his mood brightening slightly.

#

Chapter 16

Jake, Leo and Marcus stood back and looked at the summer house they had spent all day building at the northern end of the village. It was going to be used as a guard hut. A fairly basic structure, it had a set of double doors and a small glass window on the wall each side of the doors. The doors opened facing the road and gave a good view of anyone approaching.

"Needs a bit of furniture." Leo said. "Can't spend hours in it like this."

"Somewhere to sit, something to do." Marcus mused.

"We can get an armchair or two and some books maybe." Jake offered.

Jake was still upset by Connor's death. Laura's taking over had stunned him but it was a relief. She amazed him; he had told her that the night before. They had spoken for a long time, discussing events and what was needed for the future. Jake had heard everyone say it wasn't his fault but he couldn't help but blame himself. He should have gone back with them, should have spent more time training the group. He wondered if something was out to get them all, with Justin's death, then Connor's. The village should have been a safe place but more people in the group had died in the few days they had been there than had died during the rest of the time he had known them.

"I'll take first watch." Jake offered.

"You really think anyone is going to find us here?" Leo asked.

"I didn't think Connor would die on a routine walk but look how that turned out." Jake snapped back. "You two go back, I'm only staying on till last light, I doubt anyone will be out overnight."

Leo and Marcus nodded and left. Jake sat down at the entrance to the hut. He placed his rifle by his side and looked out along the road. Sentry duty, something he had done countless times during his time in the army. Part of him knew he was being stupid. Anyone wanting to attack them could come from dozens of directions. It was impossible to guard something the size of the village properly with the resources they had. The other part of him needed to do something. The sun started to set, he took another look down the road and seeing nothing new he stood up, slung his rifle and walked back to the village. He found Laura, Alex, Chloe and Timber playing in the park near the house. He went over and joined them.

#

Chapter 17

Laura looked around the room. The second daily

meeting was ready to start. Jake had missed the first one

but there hadn't been much to discuss as the day had

been spent stockpiling the supplies gathered in

Newhaven and sorting all the farm equipment.

"Right, Will, you go first." Laura opened. "Then

we can go round the room."

"The farm is well equipped. We have everything

we need. I've been and looked round the land. There is

so much space available on the east side for growing

crops. The west side is better suited for animals. We

have some sheep and cows. We could do with horses and

finding horse-drawn farming equipment as we can't use

the tractors." Will gave his report. "We have wheat and

potatoes growing, I have got a team set up growing tunnels for various fruit and veg. They should be built in the next couple of days."

"Wow, great work." Laura grinned. "Chris, the school?"

"We have five students, Alex, Chloe, Henry, George and Hattie. No issues, I could do with another teacher as Hattie is a lot older than the others but I can make it work for now." Chris answered,

"Thanks." Laura turned to the next person. "Elaine, medical?"

"Nothing to report."

"Jamal, weapon training?"

"People are getting better. I've got another ten to train tomorrow."

"Great." Laura had momentum building. "Jake,"

"Guard huts are in place. A rota is set up. I don't think there is much more I can do with it realistically." Jake started. "I'm looking at a map and figuring out other places where groups could be holding out."

"We aren't going anywhere for a while but good work."

Rob's report had been quick and easy, He had a garage that he had taken over and was set up. Jessie updated them on the food situation. They had plenty of tinned and dried food which they had collected. Her main problem was water and heating the food but they were fine for now.

"Ok Peter, saving the best for last hopefully?" Laura asked.

"We have got ideas. We are working on several composting toilets around the village. We think we can make solar power work. We would need solar panels and the batteries. That's for the future. We think we can adapt a lorry or two to run on electricity, charged from the solar panels."

"That would be amazing." She grinned.

Laura could feel the buzz in the room from the update. Everyone suddenly seemed to be a bit more upright and focused.

"It isn't going to power everything and it won't be as it was. They would be used for essentials, electric ovens, heating, electric vehicles and batteries." Peter added.

"How soon could you do it?" Laura asked.

"If we get the equipment, a week maybe, but we would need to find the solar panels and batteries first."

"Jake, add to your list. See if you can find a

phone book in the village and find solar panel fitters."

Laura ordered. "I wish google was still a thing."

#

Chapter 18

Two weeks of activity had changed a lot in the village. Jake had to admit he was impressed. Everyone now walked around with either a rifle or a shotgun. The guard huts now had a sofa and table. The toilets had been built around the village. The farm was being run, crops tended to and animals checked on. People had volunteered to run the clothing stores, help in the kitchen and assist Rob in his workshop. It was hard work but rewarding. Jake had spent time with those who wanted to scout and trained them harder. He wasn't quite ready to go out again. They needed more work but he was happier. He was now on guard duty at the northern end of the village. Since Connor's death they hadn't seen anyone else. He was starting to relax. He had a book on the table in front of him, his rifle next to it, the sun was just starting to set. He sat watching the sky change colour. The world seemed calmer. Jake stood and picked up the rifle. He left the hut and closed it. He had taken three steps towards home when he heard the sound of two gunshots in the distance, back towards the main road. He froze, listening for the next sound. Nothing. Silence. He doubted that the noise could be heard in the village. Nobody would be coming out to join him. He had a choice to make, go into the village and get some help or go and investigate by himself. Go home and forget he heard anything. He looked in the direction of the shots. No sign of anyone. He made his decision. It was only going to be a quick look round. No need to alarm everyone.

Ten minutes later he reached the roundabout on the main road between Eastbourne to the east and Lewes to the west, north to Berwick and south to the village. He hid in the shadows. No signs of anyone else. He waited. Had he imagined it? Jake wasn't sure. Then he was. A woman appeared from the north, the fading light making it hard to make out features. She was running, glancing backwards. Her clothes were torn, the exposed skin he could see covered in grime. Another woman came into view following the same path as the first. She was barefoot and limping slightly. Jake waited. Then another person came into view, holding a long barrelled weapon. Jake couldn't tell in the light what it was. The figure raised the weapon and started to take aim. Jake reacted on instinct, his rifle up and into the stance he had used thousands of times; head moving to meet the cheek piece, right eye behind the rear sight and lining up the target. He squeezed the trigger and felt the single shot leave the rifle. It slammed into the ground at the figure's feet, the roar of the shot deafening in the still evening. The figure turned and ran. The women screamed, fearing they were trapped. They moved to each other. Jake kept looking past them, making sure the figure was gone. Once he was satisfied he turned to the women.

"Who was that?" Jake asked.

"One of the brethren." The woman who had been limping replied.

"We don't know their name, they just call themselves the brethren." The other one added.

"Right, and they are?" Jake asked again, more confused than before.

"They are the ones who killed the people we were travelling with after offering us safety."

"We won't bother you; let us go. We can find somewhere to hold up."

"If you want to go I won't stop you but you'll need a weapon." Jake stated. "As you know not everyone you meet is going to be nice. I bet they said something similar but I know somewhere you can stay tonight, rest up and then move on if you want or stay if you prefer."

"We don't know you. It could be escaping one evil for another." The woman with the limp argued.

"I don't know Katy, he seems genuine." The other woman countered.

"Eliza, we need to get away, what if more of the brethren come?"

"Less than two miles from here there is a village, with about eighty survivors, who can help you." Jake explained. "I heard gunshots and came to investigate."

"I think we should go there. We can rest overnight and then leave tomorrow." Eliza said firmly. "No more talking."

#

Chapter 19

Laura was worried. Darkness had fallen and Jake still wasn't home. They hadn't been here long, he had made a point of getting home just after last light, but it was past that now. She checked that Alex and Chloe were in bed and sleeping. Timber was by her side. Laura took her rifle and grabbed a spare magazine before heading out of the front door. Timber followed. She found Jenny's house and knocked the door. Leo answered.

"Oh, I thought this was Jenny's house." Laura said surprised.

"It is. I was only visiting." Leo answered, "I was just leaving."

"Oh I didn't mean to interrupt." Laura apologised. "I can come back."

"It's fine. What can I do for you?" Jenny asked as she came into view.

"Can you watch the kids? Jake hasn't come home and I want to go look for him."

"Sure, Leo, you can help Laura look for Jake." Jenny said, grabbing her rifle.

Leo nodded and Laura led the way, Timber following. She would start at the guard hut and move out from there. They walked fast, they reached the hut and found it closed up. Leo dropped to one knee. His rifle was aimed north down the road. Laura looked around. It was dark, the stars peeped out from behind patchy clouds and there was only a sliver of moon. She couldn't see far. Jake could be dying twenty feet away and she wouldn't see him. Timber started running. He disappeared into the night. Laura and Leo froze, listening for anything in the still night air. A scrape of boot on gravel, was someone just out of sight? Laura tensed.

"Timber, calm down." Jake's voice travelled in the night.

"Jake, what's going on?" Laura questioned the night.

Jake came into view with two women level with him. One was supporting the other. They both looked worse for wear in the light they had. Leo moved past them and covered the way they had come from.

"I'll explain once we are in the village." Jake replied. "Leo, can you round up some of the scout team?"

Twenty minutes later Laura was in the community centre with Jake, the two women, Leo, Marcus, Peter and Elaine. They had a couple of lit candles for light.

"I was at the guard hut when I heard two gunshots. I decided to check out what was going on." Jake started to explain. "I found Katy and Eliza being chased by someone. I fired a warning shot and the person ran off. I offered them both somewhere safe tonight and then they can decide what they want to do in the morning."

"Who was the person?" Peter asked the women.

"One of the brethren. I don't know which one. There were four of us travelling on foot from East Grinstead towards Eastbourne, we had heard that there was a group near there we might be able to join. We thought we would cut the corner on the A22 and come out south of Hailsham. We were stopped by an old man, who seemed friendly at first. He got us talking, offered us a bed for the night and then from nowhere two more men appeared holding guns. They told us to stay still. Our friends tried to run and the men shot them. We were then forced into the house they had and locked in the basement." Katy told them all.

"We were there for about two weeks." Eliza took over. "They fed us two meals a day, they only let us out if we were tied together and they always had guns with them. One of them came to see us tonight. He was a creep, always staring at us. I hit him with the bucket we had in the basement. We then made a run for it. There were five of them that we saw."

"Where was the house?" Peter asked before Jake could.

"About a mile from the A22." Katy said, "I don't know exactly. It was near a river."

"They said that God had sent us to them so that they could save us." Eliza added. "It was an old house next to a church."

"I think I've got it." Jake said looking at a map. "Five miles from us."

Laura looked at the two women. They clearly had been through a lot. Elaine was ready to give them a quick check over.

"We will get you a place to stay tonight, you can then see what you want to do in the morning."

"Leo, Marcus, Peter, we are going to go there, see what is going on." Jake ordered.

Chapter 20

Jake had eyes on the front door of the house. The sun had started to come up an hour earlier. He had been in position for almost two hours before then. He was tired. Leo and Marcus were on the other side of building. Peter was behind Jake. They had decided to watch the house which they thought was the one the brethren were using before doing anything. The door opened and three men stepped out. Two had shotguns. The third had a hunting rifle. They walked with purpose away from the house. They disappeared around the corner of a barn. Two more men came out of the house; one was clearly a lot older than the other four. The first three came back into view. They all stood in a circle. Jake watched as they talked. The one with the hunting rifle seemed to be in trouble.

The older man slapped him hard. Peter slid alongside

Jake and they both watched events unfolding. The men

were arguing. The one with the hunting rifle stepped

back and raised it. He pulled the trigger. The old man

fell backwards, a spray of blood and soft tissue flying

from his back. The two with shotguns fired together and

the one with the hunting rifle was ripped apart by pellets.

The other man watched it all happen. The three survivors

looked at each other. It was as if the world had gone

silent. Jake and Peter exchanged a look. They both stood

up and pointed their rifles at the men. The two holding

the shotguns raised them. Jake and Peter both pulled

their triggers twice. The men with the shotguns both

collapsed immediately. The final man reached for the

hunting rifle. Jake fired again, his bullet tearing the

man's head apart. Leo and Marcus ran into view. They looked shocked at the sight of the bodies.

"Clear the buildings. Let's make sure nobody else is here." Jake ordered.

They started a sweep of the area. The barn and house were clear. No sign of anyone else. Jake stopped in a bedroom and grabbed an open notebook on a desk. Peter, Leo and Marcus were looking for anything worth taking back to the village.

They regrouped after twenty minutes. There was an outdoor seating area near the barn. Jake sat down first and the other three joined him.

"Who were they?" Leo asked. "Shame we didn't get one alive to ask them."

"I found a diary. The writer was a bit crazy from the looks of it." Jake replied, looking at the notepad.

"I warned them this would happen. Spent my days trying to get the message across. Every Saturday in town shouting the Lord's message. The virus is the Lord's work, removing the stains of society."

"Sounds like a lovely person." Peter interrupted.

"Percy and Harold are alive. The rest of the congregation are dead. Percy suggested the priory. We arrived to find it empty." Jake carried on. *"We are praying every day. We have found another of the congregation, Jasper. He's a bit odd."*

"Oh great, religion!" Leo rolled his eyes.

"The Lord has sent us another survivor. Isaac. He believes the Lord's word." Jake carried on reading out loud. *"More survivors, two women this time. Jasper has said he will look after them. Another two weren't ready to believe, so we sacrificed them."*

"Nice people, we've done the world a favour." Marcus spat.

"I hope that we start finding some normal survivors." Jake said.

#

Chapter 21

Laura was in the community centre straight after breakfast. She was making notes and looking at lists. Jenny walked in and joined Laura.

"So, Leo, how long has he been visiting?" Laura asked with a sly smile.

"He has visited a couple of times. We get on well." Jenny answered.

"Oh really, is that the new world lingo?"

"It's not like that."

"If you say so."

They both started laughing. Elaine walked in with Katy and Eliza. Both Eliza and Katy looked rested. Katy had heavy strapping around her right ankle. They looked like new people compared with the night before. They were wearing new clothes and had washed.

"Hi, how are you?" Laura asked. "Did you sleep well? Do you need anything?"

"We're good thank you. Best night's sleep in a long time." Katy replied

"Thank you, you didn't have to let us stay." Eliza carried on.

"I've been where you were. Funnily enough, Jake rescued me as well." Laura said.

"Me too." Jenny added.

"There's a recurring theme here then." Katy joked. "Is there anyone here Jake hasn't saved?"

"Erm, now that you mention it…" Laura thought about it.

They all started laughing. The mood lightened. Laura offered to show Katy and Eliza around the village. They accepted and they set off, while Jenny and Elaine stayed behind at the community centre.

"So, you said you were heading to Eastbourne?" Laura asked as they walked.

"Yeah, we were with a small group near East Grinstead. A guy we encountered talked about a group of survivors who were setting up a community there. Four of us wanted to go. Sammie and Jack were keen. Then we ran into the Brethren." Eliza explained. "Have you heard of them?"

"We were in Eastbourne until about two and a half weeks ago." Laura answered. "I guess you are looking for us?"

"Wow, really?" Katy couldn't believe it.

Chapter 22

Katy couldn't believe their luck. Finding the group they were looking for after their encounter with the religious nuts. The village was impressive. The group had clearly spent time and effort in setting things up. Eliza was just as excited to find them. The tour had been extensive. Laura had explained how Jake had rescued her and her two children from three men who had cornered them, how he had led the defence against a group of rogue survivors and then led them to the village, how others had joined the group and what they were doing to keep the community growing. They had ended back at the community centre and Laura had offered them to stay another night or longer if they wanted. They were free to leave at any time, like everyone else. Katy and

Eliza had agreed to stay another night and gone back to the house they had been shown to the night before. They sat on the sofas. Tiredness wracked their bodies.

"I think we should stay. We could offer to work in the school?" Katy suggested.

"I agree, it's nice here." Eliza nodded. "Not many children; we used to teach classes of thirty, five is easy."

Eliza got up and walked around the house. They hadn't explored it yet. When they had been let in the night before they had made it as far as the sofas before falling asleep. Eliza opened a door and gasped. She called for Katy and went in. The room was a music room. There were guitars of all types along one wall, as well as a keyboard and a drum set. Katy limped into the room and squealed with delight. Eliza felt fate was sending her a sign to stay. Before the virus, they had been starting out as country singers.

"Do you think it's a sign from Mum and Dad?" Eliza asked.

"I don't know but if it is they have sent a good one." Katy replied, picking up an acoustic guitar.

They inspected all the instruments and selected a few of the best ones before looking around the rest of the house. It had been well maintained and looked clean. There was no sign that anyone had died in the house during the virus. They each chose a bedroom and were asleep within minutes of getting into bed.

#

Chapter 23

Jake, Leo, Marcus and Peter finished going through the Brethren's diary and then buried their bodies. By lunchtime they were all exhausted. Jake hadn't slept in thirty hours, the adrenaline keeping him going. They still had to sort through everything the Brethren had stockpiled and take away anything useful.

"Can we have a nap?" Leo asked, "I am hanging."

"It's not a terrible idea." Marcus backed Leo up.

"It's not a great idea." Peter replied. "I don't disagree though."

"Let's grab an hour." Jake suggested. "We can rest properly when we get back to the village.

They each found a bed and lay down for some sleep. Jake's mind switched off before his body, as the events of the previous day began catching up with him.

They all woke up later than planned. With their bodies and minds feeling better, they searched the area and loaded food and bedding into wheelbarrows before starting their trek back to the village. They encountered nobody during their walk.

"Four guys taking wheelbarrows full of stuff they didn't pay for a year ago would have set the Facebook police into overdrive," Marcus joked. "Oh, how times have changed!"

They all laughed. Marcus wasn't wrong. They all knew it. The four of them entered the village and deposited their captured food with Jessie and the bedding in the clothing supply building. Laura met them outside the community centre.

"Hey, how did it go?" she asked.

"Complete chaos! Turns out they were extremist religious people who thought it was their mission to save people." Peter started. "One shot another one, two more shot the first and we shot them and one other."

"Basically right. It appeared to kick off with one being punished, presumably for Katy and Eliza escaping." Jake added. "We took some supplies and buried them."

"Oh wow." Laura gasped, "Are you ok?"

"All good." Leo replied.

Peter, Leo and Marcus walked off, leaving Jake and Laura alone.

"Not been much time for us to be us, has there?" Jake said. "No dates or anything."

"It's been a bit crazy." Laura agreed. "What was it people used to say, the two most stressful things in life, moving house and getting married."

"Move house, move a whole community. I guess they are similar." Jake laughed pretending to weigh them.

"Good point, we aren't doing things slowly are we?"

"No, but that's the world we are in now. How about tomorrow we take a day for us?"

"Ok." Laura agreed before kissing him. "Oh, Katy and Eliza are staying tonight. I showed them round and they said they would stay another night."

#

Chapter 24

Laura and Jake dropped Alex and Chloe at the school gates. Chloe gripped Jake's hand the entire way. Alex had Timber on a lead. Chloe made Jake promise to meet them at the end of the school day before she went in. Alex handed over Timber's lead to Laura before going in. To Jake it felt weirdly normal, walking the kids to school with a dog on a lead, like something out of a movie, if you removed the rifles slung across his and Laura's back. The ideal family dynamic. Something he had never had, growing up in care and never really having a permanent family; joining the army; moving bases on a fairly regular basis and then the virus. He smiled and took Laura's hand. They walked through the village. They had agreed a cover story if anyone asked them what they were up to, they were going on a look around the area to check the natural defences. Nobody stopped them and they made it to the edge of the village without needing to say anything, They found a sign for a public footpath and started along it.

"Do you have any idea where this leads?" Laura asked,

"The path, not a clue." Jake smiled. "Us, I have no clue."

"So funny." She retorted.

Jake let Timber off the lead to explore. Jake and Laura walked hand-in-hand along the path that led them away from the village and onto the rolling hills of the South Downs. They chatted about the village and how it was developing. The path started sloping steeply up-hill. They pushed each other on. By the time they reached the top their leg muscles were burning. Laura sat down and rubbed the back of her legs. Jake leant against a fence post.

"I swear I was fitter than this." He panted.

"Oh sure, I bet you were." Laura laughed.

Timber ran around sniffing the ground and exploring. Jake eventually sat down next to Laura and they both looked out at the views. Jake's left hand found Laura's right and they sat there in silence together for a few minutes.

"I wonder how many others are out there?" Laura asked eventually. "In the area we can see. How many people do you think are out there?"

"I have no idea, I've been looking at the map and thinking about where to look. Do we go to farms, villages, towns, remote houses? Are they friendly, hostile, wary? There are so many variables. I don't know where to start."

"Just start in one direction and go from there." Laura shrugged. "We know of a group near East Grinstead, let's head that way?"

"That sounds like a plan,"

#

Chapter 25

Jake and Laura walked back into the village late in the afternoon. There was a buzz around the village. Jenny spotted them and rushed over. She was clearly excited.

"Have you heard?" Jenny asked,

"Heard what?" Laura asked back.

"Katy and Eliza are going to put on a concert tonight." Jenny exclaimed "They were starting on a music career before the virus, and so they offered to put on a show to say thanks and raise spirits."

"Oh cool." Jake grinned. "A concert."

"Starts at seven thirty." Jenny carried on. "I haven't been to a show before."

"Where?"

"Community Centre. They've been working on it all day."

Jake and Laura nodded and rushed off to collect Alex and Chloe. By the time they sat and ate dinner it was the only subject of conversation around the village. The dining room was alive with people talking about the concert. At seven everyone was gathered outside the community centre. The buzz was incredible. At ten past the doors were opened by Jenny and everyone went in, leaving their weapons by the entrance. Leo stood with Jenny, arm in arm. Jake looked around the room and at the groups which had formed. Chris appeared on his right.

"Can you rescue a few more performers? Maybe a jazz musician, or an opera singer?" Chris grinned.

"I will try my best." Jake laughed.

At exactly half seven Eliza and Katy walked on stage with guitars slung in a similar way to how Jake would sling a rifle. The room went silent, the sense of excitement building. Laura grabbed Jake's left hand. Eliza struck the first note on the guitar and launched into a cover of 'Wildest Dreams' by Taylor Swift. When they finished, the room erupted into applause.

#

Chapter 26

Eliza was buzzing, the crowd was hyper; Katy was feeding off the energy. They kept going, song after song, covers of classics, some less well known artists and a couple of their own songs. They had discussed beforehand which songs they would perform and had done all but one, the last song of the night in a room full of people who had sung along, cheered, clapped and danced all evening.

"Thank you, we hope you had fun." Eliza shouted. "This is the last song for the evening."

"We will do this again, don't worry." Katy added.

They walked off stage after the last song and mixed with the crowd, giving and receiving high fives and handshakes. Time flew by and when they got to bed they were exhausted. It felt great to do something normal, something pre-virus. They both slept dreamless, deep sleeps that night.

Eliza and Katy had barely finished getting dressed the next day before there was a knock at their front door. Katy opened it to find Jake with a whole stack of papers. She let him in and he went to the first table he could find.

"You travelled from a group near East Grinstead?" Jake asked with an urgency they hadn't expected.

"Yes, Standen House. It was a National Trust place where about twenty of us ended up at moving to. We all were from that area." Katy answered, "Why?"

"Did you see anyone else, any signs of anyone?" Jake asked.

"No, not really." Eliza started, "We were heading for Eastbourne. The first people we actually encountered were the ones you know about."

"Did anyone in your group mention any other survivors?"

"A guy passing through mentioned you. He said he had left you and was going to head north to see if he could find some family who lived that way," Katy explained. "Why?"

"We are going to look for more survivors, to see if we can help them and they help us. So far all we've found have been people who aren't friendly."

"Oh, sorry, we haven't heard of any other groups." Eliza said.

#

Chapter 27

Three weeks passed rapidly. Between continuing the work on the farm, training for exploration trips and maintenance around the village there had been very little downtime for anyone. Chris had been moved from teaching to helping Jake since Eliza and Katy took over running the school. Jake looked at the group with him and smiled.

"Simple plan, today we walk out to Hailsham, looking for signs of life. We search for anything useful and stockpile it. There was a solar panel company listed in the phone book that had an address in Hailsham." Jake briefed them again.

"It's a three hour walk so we are going out and back in one day. We know the plan, relax." Leo quipped

Jake grinned and nodded and Leo set off. They passed the northern guard hut and headed to the main road. As Leo cut across the roundabout rain started falling. Thick heavy drops splashed onto the ground. The eight of them had waterproof jackets on and almost in unison they raised the hoods. Heads down, rifles gripped tightly, they carried on, with their clothes becoming steadily soaked. They reached their first scheduled rest point, a service area with a petrol station, hotel and fast food outlet. Judging by the weeds and general lack of attention, they guessed that nobody had been there for months. Chris took Peter, Leo and Marcus and searched the hotel for food and equipment; Jake took Hugo and cleared the petrol station, while James and Jamal did a quick sweep of the fast food outlet. Ten minutes later they linked up again. Each group passed on what they had found and then they set off again heading north to Hailsham. They reached the Diplocks roundabout and turned right, following it into the industrial estate at the western edge of town. The rain was still hammering down, beating a constant rhythm on their hoods. There was no sign of anyone having been there recently. Leo found the building which they were looking for. Marcus forced the door open and the group hurried inside. The break from the rain was pleasant. Peter started going through everything they would need to take back for the solar project. Two hours later they had stacked up piles of solar panels, cables, batteries and tools into a van which Hugo and Jamal had found and got working. Once it was loaded Hugo and Jamal drove off. The rest carried on with their search, pushing into Hailsham. The town looked deserted. The weeds that had grown up showed no signs of being flattened. Jake checked his map. They were running out of time if they were going to head back in daylight. They reached the middle of the town and carried out a quick search. Finding nothing, they took the main road back out of Hailsham and eventually returned to the services where they had stopped earlier in the day. They stopped for a quick break before pushing on. With light fading and heavy clouds above, they reached the edge of the village and went straight to the community centre. Laura, Jenni, Hugo and Jamal were there waiting.

"Good haul?" Jake asked

"It's a very good haul." Laura grinned, "Henry says he could have something set up and working in a couple of days to test the concept."

#

Chapter 28

Laura looked up at the sky, Henry had installed a solar

panel system on the roof of the community centre. It had

taken three days in the end. It had been cloudy

throughout the three days during the installation and the

weather showed no sign of improvement now that it was

installed. There was barely any charge in the system.

Jake and his scouting party were off on another search,

pushing east towards Bexhill. The plan was for them to

be away for three nights. One day to reach and search

Bexhill, the next day to skirt out to the edge of Hastings

and then north and sweep back to the villages to the

north of Bexhill, and then the final day to follow an

inland route back to the village, They had left three

hours ago, just after first light. Jake had hugged Alex and

Chloe before he left. Alex had given Jake a stuffed tiger to take with him, it was a gift Jake had given Alex not long after Jake had saved all three of them from a group of men. She looked at the calendar on the wall. Winter was coming and the group were still stockpiling and readying themselves for the weather. Laura took a deep breath and walked towards the buildings which housed most of the supplies in the village. She passed Rob's workshop and saw him hunched over a desk.

"What are you making?" Laura asked as she changed direction and approached him.

"Just finishing the circuits for the electric engine which will be going in the lorry. It will give us a way of moving large amounts of equipment." Rob shrugged. "Should be ready soon."

"Oh wow, I'd forgotten you were doing that."

"I've got a couple of other things ready to use already." Rob gestured behind him.

Laura looked at the items he had pointed out. One looked like a modern version of a wild west wagon. The other was hard to figure out. It looked like a spider with a tail. She couldn't hide her confusion.

"They work together. The wagon is for moving supplies or people. The spider mount is for bikes, we can clip different bikes onto it, attach to the wagon and then cycle away with it. Not perfect but it'll do."

"Wow, that's cool." Laura grinned.

"If we find other groups, we can use it to get to them faster and with more supplies. I reckon trading with other communities will be something that will become the new normal, money isn't really needed now."

"Does Jake know about this?"

"Not yet. I'll tell him when he gets back."

#

Chapter 29

Leo was at the front of the group. He had pretty much given up looking for signs of human life on the patrol. They had followed the main road back past Eastbourne and into Little Common. There had a been a brief talk about heading back to the caravan park for nostalgia but they had voted against it in the end. In the six hours it had taken to walk from the village to the roundabout in Little Common, Leo had seen nothing which suggested people were alive in the area. The grey skies and cold wind was eating away at everyone's morale. Leo trudged up the hill towards Bexhill. Everyone behind him moved in silence. Leo stopped at a crossroads, a fire station on his right and a school on his left. Jake gestured for him to go right. Leo led the way and they followed the road into Bexhill. Leo had taken ten steps when he froze. The person fifty metres in front of him pushing a trolley also froze. They looked at each other for what felt like a lifetime. Leo could see the shotgun resting across the trolley. He had his rifle in one hand.

"Hi there!" Leo said, instantly knowing that he would be teased for such a cliché greeting.

"Hi," a female voice responded. "If you let me go, I'll leave the trolley."

"We have no need for what is in the trolley, you are welcome to it." Leo replied, "We mean you no harm."

"How do I know that's the case?"

"You don't." Leo said before using the sling to move his rifle behind him. "I'm Leo, the others are part of a community which we have established."

"Clara," the female replied, stepping round the trolley.

"You've done well to survive this long," Leo offered. "Are you by yourself?"

"Thanks. No, we have a small community north of here in the valley." Clara answered.

Leo stood and studied her for a moment. She seemed to be in her thirties, dressed in a dark green waterproof jacket, trousers and walking boots. He couldn't see her hair under the hood of the jacket. Taking another look around, he could see signs of human life.

"Could we meet the rest of your group?" Jake asked

"Yeah, you would be the third group we've met."

#

Chapter 30

In the hour it had taken to walk to Clara's community Jake had learnt a lot about them. There were twenty in their community, most of whom lived in the middle of the village with a couple of people living just outside the village. They had all lived in the area and banded together in the aftermath of the pandemic. After a couple of problematic encounters with bandits things had become peaceful. While exploring the area they had found two more groups of survivors, one near Burwash and the other at Scotney Castle. There had been talk of another group west of Battle but Clara and her group hadn't seen anyone when they had been exploring in that direction. In return Jake explained everything that had happened to his group since the virus had hit. Clara was shocked by the details of the other group. Nobody her group had encountered had shown the same violence or behaviour that Jake described. The bandits had tried to steal supplies. One group had been killed, the other had given up quickly and joined them. Clara had told Jake her life story, an office worker before the virus. She saw her own friends and family die while she survived, then had gone searching for food and other essential resources alongside people she had barely known before and trying to adapt to the new normal.

"Welcome to Crowhurst." Clara said as they passed the sign which marked the entrance to her village. "On the left is Jeff's house. He's our sort of leader."

They carried on the tour and walked around the village before stopping at the pub. Clara led them in. Four people were sitting at a table, looking at a list, three young men and one old man. The older man stood up, a solid mass of a man, wild grey hair and a silver beard with streaks of brown. Clara introduced them to each other.

"Jake, this is Jeff. Jake is from a group in Alfriston." Clara began, "Leo, Marcus, Peter, Hugo, James, Jamal and Chris. They were exploring the area trying to find survivors. I found them near Aldi in Bexhill."

"Good to meet you." Jeff said, shaking everyone's hand. "I see you are well prepared."

"Good to meet you too," Jake grinned. "We have had some problems with rogue survivors. Can't be too careful these days."

"Understandable. We had some problems ourselves."

"Clara did mention some issues; she also said that you found some friendly groups."

"We have. Take a seat. I think we have lots to discuss."

Everyone sat down and the two groups swapped stories of survival and discussed challenges they had faced and were still facing. Light started to fade and Jeff offered Jake and the others use of a house to stay overnight. They accepted and went to settle down for the night.

#

Chapter 31

Leo woke up and rolled over. He fell off the sofa he had been sleeping on and thudded onto the floor. It took him a moment to remember where he was. The others were spread throughout the house. Jeff had let them use one of the larger houses in the village. Leo listened as the rain outside thumped into the windows and wind roared over the top. Leo packed his sleeping bag into his rucksack and walked around the house. It had clearly belonged to someone wealthy. He stopped and admired some of the artwork on the walls. Under one portrait of a man in military uniform he spotted a table with magazines and catalogues on it. He grabbed one, a brochure about military kit.

"Anything good in there?" Jake asked, appearing in the doorway to the room.

"A lot which is probably useful now." Leo replied

"We are going to leave soon. Are you ready to go?"

Leo nodded and Jake walked away. Leo continued looking through the catalogue, then went back to his rucksack and put his waterproofs back on. Once everyone was ready, Jake gathered the group together. There was a change of plans. Jake briefed them all and everyone agreed. Leo was going to be point again. The change called for a full day of walking. Leo led the way. The rain had stopped, the wind had died down, but the weather was freezing. Clara was leaving her house as Leo led the group out of the village.

"Come back any time. We are happy to swap items and knowledge," Clara said as Jake explained their departure. "Maybe we'll come and visit you as well?"

"Thanks we will come back. We are going to head home now and let our people know what we found." Jake replied as they headed off.

Leo followed the road signs. His first checkpoint on their journey was in Battle. They reached the town square outside the Abbey and looked for somewhere to shelter from the wind. Leo kicked open a door to a shop and everyone rushed inside. The air was damp and musty, but a break from the wind was welcome, They all took a swig from their water bottles and then Jake gave the order to move on. Leo summoned the courage to go back out and carry on the walk. He tried to imagine being home with Jenny in the warmth. They hadn't agreed to anything official. They hadn't defined what they were.

Leo continued walking. He knew to head towards Heathfield as that was the next checkpoint. During the entire walk his mind was trying to process what was going on with him and Jenny. Four hard energy-sapping hours later up and down hills, Leo led the group into Heathfield. The light was already fading as heavy grey clouds filled the sky. Jake looked at everyone in the group and told Leo to pick a house to break into and get them into shelter. Leo went to the closest house, a detached house on a corner with a paved and pebbled front garden. He was about to break the window by the door when Marcus tapped him on the shoulder and pointed. There was a lock box for a key on the wall. Marcus grabbed a rock from the garden and smashed it open before handing Leo the key. Leo let everyone in and closed the door behind them. Almost instantly the group spread out around the house. Leo put his rucksack down next to a sofa. He ached, having realised how cold he had become on the walk. He placed his rifle down and took his waterproofs off. Looking round the room he saw an open fireplace with a stack of logs by it. Leo stumbled over, placed a few logs in the fireplace and then scrambled around in his bag for a lighter. He found it and managed to get it lit. He grabbed a piece of paper from the coffee table and managed to get a corner burning. He placed it on the logs and started to pray that it started the fire.

"Guys, in here!" Leo shouted, "I've got a fire going."

#

Chapter 32

Jake was the last one into the room, the log fire was warming the room and everyone sat around it. He had looked around the house and found a basement. He had found crates of beer down there and brought a crate up with him. He handed everyone a beer before closing the door to the room and sitting down. Chris used a Swiss army knife to open his beer and then handed it round for everyone else to use.

"To surviving," Jake offered, raising his glass.

Everyone repeated it and took a swig of beer. Nobody spoke for a few moments, but sat enjoying the moment, mulling over the journey so far.

"Is it me or does Autumn seem harsher this year?" Chris asked breaking the silence.

"Bloody hell, the world ended and still we Brits talk about the weather." Jamal grinned.

"Some things will never change." Jake added

They carried on talking and making jokes, more beers were passed round and everyone's mood lifted. Jake and Leo were the last ones left standing. Everyone else had gone to bed at different times.

"Jake, how do you keep going?" Leo asked, "I mean you've got it sorted back in the village with Laura, Chloe, Alex, a family, and you could just stay there with them but you keep coming out here with us."

"I've never had a family. I grew up in care and I'm still adjusting to it. I was in the forces, moved around, my longest relationship was with my care home staff and that changed regularly." Jake began, "The idea of being in one place, of being down is alien to me. Before the virus I had no plans to meet someone, never thought a family was likely."

"Oh." Leo said

"It scares me but in a good way. I leave them because I know what I'm doing is for them."

"Makes sense." Leo nodded, "What about when Justin passed away, you seemed to avoid taking over?"

"I'm not a leader in that sense. I never wanted to be responsible for everyone," Jake replied honestly. "I haven't got a clue about all this survival stuff, things like how to run a village. You're asking lots of questions tonight."

"Just trying to make sense of things."

"Jenny?" Jake grinned, "What's the score there?"

"We are spending a lot of time together."

"Is that the post virus lingo?" Jake teased.

"I like her, I think she likes me."

"When we get back, you should talk to her, find out what is going on. Didn't she turn sixteen a couple of weeks ago? I'm off to bed, sleep well."

Jake left Leo with his thoughts. Jake collapsed on the bed which he was sharing with Chris. He crawled into his sleeping bag and placed his head on the pillows.

#

Chapter 33

Jenny took her usual seat in the community centre. Her head was spinning and she felt as if she was going to be sick again. She tried to focus on the paperwork in front of her. There was an updated list of all the food they had stockpiled. They were still well-stocked for tinned and packet food. Fresh food had been hard to come by. Plans were in place for fruit and vegetables for next year. Will and those working on the farm had worked tirelessly to get things planted. Jenny tried to compose her thoughts, check maps and lists. Laura came in and said hello. Jenny went to respond but all that came out was a stream of vomit. Fortunately, it landed in the metal bin that Jenny had by her desk. Jenny stayed hunched over the bin. Laura ran over and held Jenny's hair back. Eventually the vomiting stopped and Jenny was able to sit upright again. She wiped her mouth and then looked up at Laura.

"Are you ok?" Laura asked

"Yeah, just a bit of a bug," Jenny replied weakly.

"Are you sure that's all it is?"

"Yes, I'm sure."

"Ok, but if it carries on then please let me or Elaine know."

Jenny agreed and Laura walked away. Jenny's mind was racing. Was it just a bug or could it be something else? She shook her head and continued working. She hoped she would feel better in a couple of days, that what she had was indeed a bug, or perhaps nerves about Leo being away. He was due back later. She was trying to decide if she would ask him to make their relationship official, she hadn't had the courage to ask him what their kiss recently had meant and he hadn't asked.

By the time the light was too poor for Jenny to work she was feeling better. She joined everyone for the evening meal and then went home. She let herself in and flopped onto the sofa. She curled up with a blanket over her. Leo would be back soon. She realised that she had fallen for him in their time together.

#

Chapter 34

Jake woke up with a pounding headache. Chris's snoring next to him only made it worse. His body ached. He shrugged the sleeping bag off and got up slowly, his joints creaking as he straightened up. He made his way downstairs and joined Peter and Jamal who were in the kitchen. He looked out of the window and did a double-take. His brain refused to believe what his eyes were telling him. There was a layer of snow on the ground. He could only guess at the depth but it looked to be ankle deep. Peter and Jamal were both viewing the snow in disbelief as well. Twenty minutes later, everyone was awake and had seen the change to the landscape outside.

"Well, that's a bit shit." Chris stated with a grin. "I guess snow days aren't a thing anymore."

"We have two choices, push on to our destination or return home," Jake said. "We have no way of knowing if the snow is as far south as the village or not."

"Can we wait an hour or two, see if it melts?" Marcus asked

"Gets my vote, I'd forgotten how much hangovers suck." Peter replied.

There were murmurs of agreement from everyone. They all packed their rucksacks ready to leave before going back to their seats from the night before and lighting the fire again. They chatted about the weather and how it was snowing earlier than they had seen it for a long time. Two hours turned into three and eventually Jake said they had to leave. Everyone put their waterproofs on and they let the fire die before setting out. The snow hadn't melted. Jake took the lead, but progress was slow. The snow crunched underfoot. It was strange seeing the roads and paths covered in untouched snow. They saw no signs of human life. They did spot some animal tracks in the four hours which it took them to cover most of the walk to their destination. They had to stop for a rest, sheltering in a church to get out of the cold. They huddled together for warmth. By the time they went outside again, the light of the sun had been replaced by moonlight. Jake took the lead, convinced his navigation was right but also wishing he had access to google maps to make sure. Thirty minutes later they reached the destination. Jake gave instructions and everyone spread out. Jake approached with Leo and Marcus behind him. There was a set of stairs leading to the entrance. Jake went up first, reached the switchback on the stairs and carried on before slipping.

147

Chapter 35

Laura woke up to an empty bed again. She was starting to feel nervous. The scout party were late. It didn't mean anything bad had happened but she was worried. Jake had told her several times that they would stick to the plans unless something dramatically changed, making them no longer workable. Alex and Chloe both asked when Jake was due back. She explained it would be soon and hoped it was true. Once she had dropped them at school, she rounded up Will, Rob, Jenny and Hugo.

"Jake and the others are late. How long do we give it before we go looking for them?" Laura asked

"At least until the end of tomorrow, Will stated calmly. "They might have found a group or two. Could have found something too good to miss out on."

"If they aren't back at the end of tomorrow then, we shall have to get another party to go look for them." Rob agreed.

"We don't know where they are, where they actually went or if they are lost, on the way back or if they have been captured or killed." Hugo reasoned, "Any search party would be looking for eight needles in a hay mountain."

"We can't just leave them out there though." Jenny said angrily, "What if they need help?"

"Wait until tomorrow evening. If they aren't back, we get a team together and we go hunting for them." Will stated, ending the debate.

Nobody wanted to argue any further. Will, Rob and Hugo went back to their jobs. Laura and Jenny walked to the edge of the village with Timber behind them. They stopped by the guardhouse and found a place to sit. They watched the road and listened to the birds without talking.

"We should put a team together to start looking," Jenny said eventually. "We know the rough area they were going to. We could follow the main roads, and set a time limit of three days."

"Will is right. We shouldn't rush into anything. If they aren't back by tomorrow evening we will get a team and begin searching." Laura answered, "I don't want to wait that long but what if we go rushing off to look and the minute we are out of view one way they appear from the other way, having done something unexpected?"

The day passed slowly, the grey clouds and cold wind only adding to the tension. The guards came and went. Some tried to engage Laura and Jenny in conversation. The sun disappeared below the horizon and they both headed back. Eliza and Katy were looking after Alex and Chloe. Will had told them what was happening and, before he had finished talking, Eliza had volunteered to look after them.

#

Chapter 36

Leo looked at the stacks of equipment along the shelves and compared it with the brochure he had taken from the house in Crowhurst. There was far more than he had expected The piles of clothing, footwear and equipment which they had stacked up would keep a lot of people going for years. It had taken most of the day to collect everything deemed to be of use. Another night of sleeping in the building was lined up. They had looked for vehicles which still worked but everything was dead. They had come up with a revised plan; Leo and Marcus would stay and guard the supplies, while the others walked back to the village to get the lorries and return to collect everything.

Light was fading fast and everyone was feeling the exertion of the last few days. They had made the decision to keep all torches off and hide the fact they were there just in case anyone else came along. Given how much time had passed since the virus, they doubted that anyone would turn up suddenly but they wanted to stay safe. Leo settled down into the area he had picked to sleep and tried to get comfortable. His mind went back to Jenny, how fast things had happened since their first conversation. He had sat down next to her in the dining hall in Alfriston. He hadn't noticed her when they were in the caravan park. There had been a space on her table and he had asked if he could sit down. She had said yes, and that had been the end of the conversation. They had both eaten in silence. Leo had thought about trying to start a conversation but couldn't come up with anything to say. The next evening, he had sat down on her table again. She had been reading a book. He had recognised it as something he had been told to read at school but had watched the film instead and based his homework on the film rather than the book. He had asked her if it was any good. Jenny had looked up and shrugged and said the film was better. Leo had laughed and explained how he had ended up with a week of detentions for basing his homework on the film instead of the book. Jenny had laughed back. The conversation then flowed and Jenny told him that he could borrow the book when she had finished with it. A few nights later she had come in with it and handed him the book. He had sat and actually read it over a week.

After Connor had been killed, Jenny had offered Leo a space at her table again. She had started the conversation about what had happened. As they finished eating, Jenny had said something about Leo coming to look at the books in her house, to see if there was anything else he wanted to read. He had gone round that evening and they had looked through the previous owner's book collection. Jenny had suggested the first Harry Potter book after Leo had let slip that he had never read them or seen the films. He had taken it and started reading. Over the next two weeks he read all of them, borrowing each from Jenny. After he had read the last one, they had started talking about what they thought had happened to the characters after the book series ended. Sitting on the sofa at Jenny's one night discussing books, Jenny had moved closer to Leo, who had been reading aloud. Leo remembered everything about that evening. She had brushed her back behind her ears. She had been in jeans and black t-shirt. She had been engrossed in his words. When the time came for him to leave she had shown him to the door. He had said goodbye and Jenny had offered a hug. Leo had accepted and they shared a hug. The next night Jenny had found a copy of a play and suggested they read it together. Again they had hugged at the end of the night. The third night they continued with the play. He was going to leave, the hug had turned into a kiss. Just a simple peck on the lips. The next day there had been no mention of it and they had both acted like nothing had happened the night before leaving. Leo more confused, he had planned to ask her about it but the timing hadn't been right, hesitant to ask because he did not want to lose her as a friend. She was the last thought he had before he fell asleep.

Chapter 37

Jenny was wrapped up against the cold wind. She had decided to ignore the plan to wait until the end of the day. She had woken up just after first light and chosen to go looking. She wrote a note and left a map with her route drawn on it. She had grabbed some food from the dining hall and filled several bottles of water from the collectors on her house. With her rucksack full, she set off out of the village to the roundabout. By the time she stopped for lunch she was close Little Common. She stopped in a bus shelter, using it as wind-break. She was starting to doubt her decision but she knew she couldn't just go back. The shotgun she was carrying on her rucksack was starting to feel like a lead weight. After a brief lunch she carried on. Without knowing it she followed the same route Leo and the others had done

four days before. She stopped at the same crossroads, but

instead of turning right to go into Bexhill, she kept going

on straight over and uphill along the dual carriage way

towards Hastings. She kept going until she reached the

Harley Shute Junction. Ignoring the retail parks she

passed on way, the possibility of there being resources

wasn't enough to stop her. She had been checking her

map often and at Harley Shute she knew that she had to

turn left and go up hill. She had been looking for signs of

life and had seen nothing.

At the top of the short sharp hill Jenny paused,

looking around and seeing the light starting to fade. She

had no idea where to stay or how to get into a house. It

dawned on her how stupid it had been to go off by

herself. She decided to continue walking. She had barely

gone two hundred metres when she saw the entrance to a caravan park. In her mind she had two choices: go in to find somewhere to sleep or keep going and hope there was somewhere better. She decided to go in and find somewhere to rest overnight. Passing the barrier she moved slowly. She tried doors to buildings but found them locked. Eventually, as the light was almost gone, she found a caravan with the door unlocked. She went in and locked it behind her. Finding the bedroom she lay down on top and pulled her duvet from the rucksack. Her mind was trying to come up with a reason why Leo and the others hadn't come back. She had gone through the books in the bookshop in Alfriston and found a series for Leo to try. She thought back to their last evening together. They had read together, neither of them mentioning the kiss. She regretted not talking about it, It had been an impulse, she hadn't told many people about

her birthday, the kiss had been her way of celebrating it.

Sixteen, the world had changed beyond all imagination

in the year since her fifteenth birthday. She wondered

what the next year would bring. Her mind went back to

Leo as she drifted off to sleep.

#

Chapter 38

Jake set off early with the five others. They moved as fast as they could with the kit they had since the snow had melted away. They map had given them two routes, one back the way they had come and the other way out towards to a major road and following it back before cutting down to Berwick and into Alfriston. Jake had decided to take the second route. Everything was deserted, they reached Uckfield quickly and then joined the main road which ran all the way to Eastbourne. The roads were littered with dead branches and mounds of leaves. Jake was in the lead. As they passed through a wooded area, Jake froze. Ahead was a herd of deer. The idea of killing a couple crossed his mind but he knew he was already two days late and carrying the deer would slow them down. They moved on. By the time they reached the junction to Berwick the group were all breathing hard. They stopped for lunch. Fortunately, the warehouse had contained military style rations. The break was a welcome relief. Jake was the first to put his kit back on and they all followed his example. It took another two and half hours to get to Alfriston. Jake immediately went to find people to move the vehicles, He found Rob in his workshop and asked him what they had which still worked.

"One Sprinter van, we've got diesel from the farm for it. Two tractors but they are needed here. I've got a lorry that runs on electric. I've rigged a couple of solar panels to the roof to keep it charged as much as possible. Don't expect it to be fast but it'll do the job."

Rob explained, "I've also got a bike and trailer system rigged for eight bikes. It'll pull a fair bit."

"Awesome, we'll need them all." Jake said, "Let's go."

Peter took the sprinter van, Jamal the electric lorry and Rob joined Jake, Chris, James and Elliot in the back of the sprinter. The drive back took an hour. Light was fading, so that by the time they pulled into the car park of the warehouse in Crowborough they had the headlights on. Leo and Marcus met them. Marcus had found a hand crank for the steel shutters. They pulled both vehicles in close before working as fast as they could to load everything. When everything was loaded, they closed the shutters and then found space to get back in the vehicles. The drive back to Alfriston seemed to take forever but at the same time went by quickly. As they parked up and Jake jumped out, Laura appeared. She hugged him tight before hitting him.

"You are two days late, with no communication." She shouted.

"We had a change of plan. We have lots to discuss." Jake tried to explain.

"Yeah and your change of plan has led to a bigger issue. Jenny has gone off by herself to look for you all."

Jake saw Leo's head snap up at that comment.

#

Chapter 39

Laura hadn't thought much about Jenny is not turning up as she often went round the village checking on things in the morning, but, when she hadn't shown up midafternoon and hadn't been seen at lunch, Laura went to her house and found the note and the map. She swore. Their problems were now doubled, two sets of people out to look for. She went and found Will and explained the situation.

"Bloody hell, what was she thinking?" Will groaned

"She's close to Leo. I don't know how close. Jake saved her life. I think she thinks she owes him."

"All she had to do was wait." Will answered. "We could have sent people tomorrow. Hell, two groups, one going each way round the route to find them and meeting in the middle."

"She left a map of her route. We could go after her."

"Send more people to chase more people? When would we stop?"

Laura sighed and agreed.

"If she isn't back in three days, we will go after her, unless Jake and the others are back sooner."

"OK."

Laura went back to the community centre, looking at the map and trying to judge how far Jenny could have gone in the time she had been away. The sound of vehicles passing by caught her attention and she ran out in time to see the Sprinter van and lorry heading out of the village.

"It was Jake and the others, They've found a huge stash of equipment, they've gone to collect it." Jessie explained "He stuck his head through the door to ask where everyone was."

"He could have told me."

"He was looking for you, to give you the update."

Laura was angry with him but she also knew that if he was so deep into the mission it must be important. Jessie agreed to watch Alex and Chloe while Laura waited for the group to get back.

By the time the vehicles got back, her anger had simmered down to annoyance. Jake was barely on the ground before she hugged him and then hit him.

#

Chapter 40

Leo's head snapped up as he heard that Jenny had gone to look for them. Laura and Jake both looked towards him. His heart was beating faster. He could feel himself getting nervous. Laura and Jake gestured to him to come over.

"We have a map; we know where she is planning to go." Laura started.

"Then let's go." Leo shouted. "She's sixteen, it wasn't safe for her to be out alone before the virus; it's definitely not safe now."

"The lorry is almost out of charge; the van is virtually out of fuel." Jake began

"Then I'll walk. I'm going." Leo spat. "Give me the map."

Leo looked at Jake and Laura. He was burning with rage. If Jake had stuck to the plan they would have been back, and Jenny wouldn't have gone off and be in danger. It was Jake's fault. Leo went to swing a punch at Jake. Jake blocked it and countered with a punch to Leo's solar plexus, the air bursting from his mouth and doubling him up. Jake kept Leo on his feet.

"We will fix this. We will go after her. It's late. We've had a long day. Get your head down. Up at first light. Four of us will go after her. We will take bicycles." Jake said calmly.

"We know where she said she was going. Follow her route, you'll find her fast." Laura added.

Leo nodded in agreement. Jake sent everyone to bed, the unloading could wait. He walked Leo back to Leo's house. Leo had calmed down, by now he could understand why Jake had made the decision to loot the warehouse. It had made sense. It wouldn't have been an option if Leo hadn't found the brochure, since they wouldn't have known it was there. Jake told Leo again to be ready at first light. Leo nodded and went to bed. He was barely through the door before he was unpacking his rucksack and sorting through his gear to make it lighter. He piled it by the stairs and went to the sofa to sleep. He lay down and closed his eyes, exhaustion washing over him and sending him straight to sleep..

#

Chapter 41

Jake was running on fumes. He had no energy left. He barely got through his own front door before his legs gave out. Laura helped him to the sofa. She joined him and cuddled up into him.

"So, what happened. Talk me through it." Laura asked with her head against his chest.

"We had walked to Bexhill when we found a woman out by herself. Leo opened the conversation with her. She was with a group in Crowhurst. They have had a lot fewer problems compared with us. She invited us to meet her group. We went, started chatting, they are open to trading. They've got a setup which grows food and they are also hunting rabbits, pigeons and fish. Their leader, Jeff, invited us to stay the night. Leo found a brochure for a company in Crowborough which sold survival and military equipment. I'd forgotten about the place until I saw the brochure. I'd been to the camp in Crowborough a couple of times before the virus and to the place itself once. I made the call to head there. We were told about another group near Burwash. I thought about going there first but the warehouse was too good to pass up. The place will keep us stocked for years with footwear and clothes. It took two days to get there. We stopped in Heathfield, overnight it snowed, and the third day was a tough walk." Jake explained, "We had a few beers in Heathfield. We reached the warehouse and the light was gone so we went to sleep. Day four we spent packing anything useful and then tried to find vehicles that worked. Nothing did, we slept and then this morning we pushed hard to get back here. We went back, collected everything and have returned."

"Wow, you packed a lot in then." Laura said

The sound of Jake's heavy breathing was the only answer. He had fallen asleep right there after finishing his story. Laura had more questions, many more. She pulled a blanket over them both and stayed curled up into him. She was trying to process what she had learned about more survivor groups, people who were friendly. She had been all for heading out to Standen but, knowing there were groups the other way as well, gave her more hope.

#

Chapter 42

Jenny woke up; her body was sore. She ate
breakfast quickly and got ready to move. The thought of
Leo needing her somewhere kept her going. She started
walking inland, away from Harley Shute Hill and
following her map. She dug deep into her reserves. She
reached Battle by lunchtime. Her muscles ached as she
paused in the open square, She heard a loud bang to her
left. She ducked and turned around, a door was blowing
in the wind. She could see the lock was broken. She
grabbed her shotgun from her rucksack and kept moving,
wary that someone had been through recently. She
walked fast, straight out of Battle and along a road which
her map said would meet another road she could follow
all the way to Hailsham. She walked hard for an hour.

Eventually she reached a point where she couldn't walk any further. She looked around and saw nobody. The view despite the cold air was impressive: looking out over a small valley on one side of the road, the other was woodland, with a high brick wall and gates in the middle, although judging by the overgrowth in front of the gates, they hadn't been opened for a long time. She put her rucksack down and sat on it, her shotgun on the floor at her feet. She looked at the view across the valley, her mind wandering away. No sign of anyone apart from the banging door. She wondered where had Leo, Jake and the others got to? Why hadn't she seen any sign of them on her walk? Should she have gone through the middle of Bexhill? Her mind was still trying to think of what could have happened. Ten minutes later, she didn't hear the person sneaking up behind her. The first she knew about it was when a gloved hand went across her mouth

and another went around her neck.

#

Chapter 43

Marcus woke Leo up swiftly with a slap to the
face. Leo looked around as his brain processed where he
was and what had happened.

"It's just before first light. Get your stuff together
bro." Marcus said.

"Thanks." Leo replied groggily.

Leo rolled onto his feet and stood up. His body
felt heavy. He shook his head to clear the tiredness and
began taking some slow steps. Marcus was already at the
front door. Leo followed, grabbing his rucksack and
swinging it on to his back. They walked through the
village and to Rob's workshop. He was already there
working. He had four bicycles on stands and a bag next
to them

"Four bikes, all set and ready to go. Spare inner tubes and pumps in this bag." Rob explained, "We don't have tyres but you can probably steal those."

"Thanks, Rob." Leo said.

Jake and Chris arrived a minute later. Chris looked fine, but Jake looked tired and was moving slowly. They all chose a bicycle and took it for a quick test. Jessie stopped them as they passed her and she put food into each of their rucksacks. Laura, Alex and Chloe waved them off as they left, Timber sitting by Laura's feet. Cycling at a steady speed, they made rapid progress along the same route that they had used less than a week before. They were looking for any signs of Jenny. By the time they reached Bexhill they were all breathing hard and needing a break. They stopped at the crossroads where they had turned off before. All four of them leaned their bikes against railings and tried to stretch their aching muscles. Leo was the first back on the bike. Saddle sore and with burning legs, he led the way towards Hastings. The map showed that Jenny planned to turn off at Harley Shute. When they reached the bottom of the hill they all dismounted.

"Screw cycling up that." Jake panted.

"We can't be that far behind her." Leo said.

"Let's stop for lunch. We are going much quicker than she would on foot." Chris said. "We can be to halfway to Hailsham before the light fades."

"We are going to find her, Leo, and we are going to bring her back." Jake promised.

#

Chapter 44

The words sounded hollow to Jake even though he was trying his best to believe them. Finding one person who could easily have gone off route as they had or changed plans was almost impossible. They ate lunch, crackers and tinned meat, sitting against the wall of a house, using it as a windbreak. As soon as they were finished they got moving. At the top of the hill they got back on the bikes and carried on cycling. They passed the caravan park and headed north with Jake at the back They kept moving. Legs were pumping hard. The cold wind was numbing them. They reached Battle and stopped at the same shop as before. Jake sat with his back against a wall and closed his eyes. He was tired. The others all sat down too. The look on their faces showed the pain they were in, the tiredness they were feeling and the determination to keep going until they found Jenny. Jake had tried to calculate where on the route they would find her. His best guess would have been before they reached Battle, but they hadn't seen any sign of her. Had she been moving faster than Jake expected? Was she just a little bit further down the road? The ten minute stop turned into thirty. Summoning their strength they all went back out into the cold air and climbed on the bikes. Leo was in front. They rode into the wind all the way out of Battle. They passed the turning that they had taken to head to Heathfield and continued following the road which would spit them out between Ninfield and Hailsham. Thirty minutes later they came out of a series of bends and onto a long, straight road with a small valley on their left and woodland on their right. They passed a brick-wall with gates in the middle which looked like as if it had not been accessed for a long time. They rode past. Jake's mind noted something at the side of road but he didn't process it properly until he was half a mile down the road. By the time he reached the junction with the Ninfield to Hailsham road, his mind was screaming at him.

"Stop. We need to go back." Jake announced, "Secure the bikes out of sight. We need to walk back. Tactically."

#

Chapter 45

Laura had hated seeing Jake go away again so soon. Despite living together, they had spent barely any quality time together for a while. Alex and Chloe had both asked when Jake would be back again and she had told them it would be soon. She had no idea if it was a lie. Jake had slept soundly and had needed to be woken up. He had looked in on Alex and Chloe, seeing them both asleep before he had left. He had hugged her tight and promised that he would be back within two days. She had got Alex and Chloe up and at the side of the road, so that they could see Jake leave. School had been closed for the day, Eliza and Katy saying that the kids had been working hard day after day without a break. Laura had decided they could help with the unloading of the equipment brought back by Jake and the others.

Timber followed Laura, never more than twenty feet

away. They reached the spot where the lorry and van had

been parked overnight and could see a group already

unloading items. Rob and Peter were making lists of

clothing, footwear, headwear and other items and

directing where they should be stored. Laura tried to get

involved but Rob asked her to stay out of the way as they

had a system which worked well already. Alex and

Chloe wanted to help but again Rob said they couldn't

help just yet, but once the equipment was off and into the

stacks they could join in. Several different piles were

forming. By the time the vehicles were empty and the

stacks built up they had filled four pieces of paper front

and back. Laura looked at it all, uniforms, warm layers,

waterproofs, gloves, hats, boots. knives, rucksacks,

sleeping bags. The list went on. She was given orders by Will where to move stuff with Alex and Chloe's help. The distraction worked, she found herself thinking less about Jake and the others, even Jenny, whether they would meet each other or whether they wouldn't. Walking back and forth multiple times and stacking items neatly by type was boring but just what she needed. The weather turned from cold to bitterly cold with rain in early afternoon. They had to double their pace to get all the items out of the rain and stored. By dinner she could feel the need to stop and rest. Alex and Chloe were both getting irritable and tired. They ate with everyone and then returned home. Alex and Chloe tried to protest and stay up, in case Jake came home, but Laura firmly told them to go to bed and that she would wake them if Jake came back.

Chapter 46

Leo's mind was on overdrive. They had stowed the bikes. Jake had explained what he had seen; overgrown grass flattened, a metal and wooden object part covered by the flattened grass. It must have been recent. He had shown them where they were on a map. The four of them had then set off using the hedgerow separating the road from the fields as cover. They had no idea if anyone was following them on the road side. They moved cautiously. Rifles were moved from rucksacks to hands. They were getting close to where Jake thought he had seen the object in the grass. Leo was in front, his eyes scanning for any sign of people. Jake gave the gesture to stop. Everyone froze. Leo watched Jake shrug his rucksack off and then drop to his stomach.

Jake used his hands to push the base of the hedge apart. It took a little time but eventually there was enough space for Jake to ease through. It was tight but he disappeared through the gap he had made. Five minutes later, Jake reappeared. He had a shotgun in his right hand and he pushed it through ahead of himself. He then stayed low and took out his map. Jake looked around, making notes and drawing on the map. Leo could tell that Jake was up to something serious. Without warning, Jake gestured for them to start moving back the way they had come. Nobody spoke until they returned to the bikes. Leo was looking at the shotgun; he recognised some of the carving on the stock: it was the one Jenny had been given. He looked at Jake for an answer which he knew he didn't want to hear. Jenny knew about keeping her weapon close to her. She wouldn't leave it lying around.

Leo felt his knees go weak. He started shaking, tears welled in his eyes and his lips trembled. Something had happened to her. In that moment he couldn't see any other reason that she would leave her shotgun. He knew it was his fault. He should have come back sooner, on time even. Marcus grabbed Leo and guided him to the ground. Leo sat hunched over, tears silently running down his face. Jake sat down opposite him, mirroring Leo's position.

"Leo, look at me." Jake said firmly.

"We should have come back on time." Leo replied quietly while raising his eyes to Jake's.

"There are a million little things that could have happened differently, any one of them done a different way and this would have been a different story." Jake answered, "What matters now is how we deal with it.

We could search the area ourselves. We could go back and get help. We could walk away and never come back."

"I'm not leaving until I know what happened." Leo snapped back

"Neither are we. I'm no expert. I think whatever happened was not long before we arrived, an hour or two at most." Jake carried on, "We found her here. The only buildings close by are this one and that one."

"We could search both."

"Clara said there was talk of a group in this particular area. This one makes more sense." Jake pointed to one. "It's inside the walled area. We have an hour till last light. We go in at darkness. And we find places to hole up and then we observe."

"What about getting help?" Chris asked

"We should get some support," Marcus added. "I want to go in but at the same time we don't know how many if any are in there."

"With the best will in the world we won't get back before the light goes." Jake replied.

"So, we do this alone?"

"Leo and I will go forward. Marcus and Chris you are going to stay here. Take it in turns to sleep. I want you to go back to the village at first light, round up a team and bring them back here. Leo and I will move out under the cover of darkness and come back. If we find anyone, we can go in. If we don't, then we'll search the area a little more."

"Ok, let's get this going."

Leo was determined to make it right. They ate

another meal of tinned meat and crackers. Afterwards

they changed into dark clothing and got ready to move in.

#

Chapter 47

Jake was ahead of Leo. The light was almost

non-existent. Cloud obscured most of the stars. They

reached the area where Jake had found the shotgun and

they stopped, listening intently for anything unusual.

After hearing nothing for ten minutes they continued,

along the hedgerow and found a place to go through and

cross the road. They moved into the woodland slowly,

stopping regularly and checking for any signs of

movement. The woodland gave way to open land. Jake

and Leo stopped and dropped to their stomachs. Through

the limited light, they could see a large building on the

other side of a lake. They stayed in position and watched

for movement. There was nothing for over an hour and

then Leo thought he saw movement at ground level,

though Jake didn't see anything. They still waited. Jake slowly checked his watch, the hands telling him it was almost midnight. He gestured to Leo and they moved back into the woodland. All of the tiredness Jake had been feeling had now melted away, the adrenaline coursing through him.

"We need to be sensible and do nothing stupid." Jake said quietly.

"What's the plan?" Leo asked

"We take it in turns to watch for movement, while the other sleeps. We need to find somewhere concealed to stay during the day."

Leo nodded and they moved slowly, looking for somewhere to shelter. Eventually they found a fallen tree with enough space for them crawl under and use for cover. They could see two sides of the building from where they were. Leo volunteered for first watch and Jake accepted. He pulled his sleeping bag out of his rucksack and wriggled into it. He closed his eyes and tried to sleep. His mind drifted back to Laura, Alex and Chloe. He needed to spend more time with them. Laura would give him hell if he was late back again. He hoped that they would find Jenny and be able to return home soon.

Leo woke him up; Jake didn't remember falling asleep. The first rays of daylight were appearing in the sky. Jake looked at what Leo had woken him for. There were two people in the doorway to the building looking out over the lawns and lake. A third, smaller one appeared carrying a metal tin. Leo and Jake watched as the figure walked slowly along the path that ran round the building and then stopped at a set of steps that appeared to go down into an area below the building.

The figure went down the steps, disappeared from view

and reappeared a few minutes later, with the tin still in

his hand, and returned via the same route before

disappearing from view.

#

Chapter 48

The cold, dark, damp and dirty room she had
been dumped in was the perfect place to brood and build
up anger. Jenny was raging at herself. She should have
paid more attention to her surroundings rather than the
view. She had tried to fight off the person who had
grabbed her. She had dragged her rucksack with her feet
and seen the shotgun get partly covered with grass as she
tried to hook it. She had then been dragged to the road
and another person had taken her rucksack. Despite her
best attempts to break free, she had been tied by the arms
and legs and carried away. They had gone into the
woodland near where she had been sitting. Her mind was
racing: who had taken her and what did they want?
Would this be it? Would they kill her or would they do

worse before killing her? They had kept going, deeper into the woods. Suddenly the trees above disappeared and they were in open terrain. One of her captors looked young, maybe her age, maybe slightly older. The other one, the one who had grabbed her, had tried to stay out of sight. She had caught glimpses. They were older, serious looking. Jenny thought it may have been a woman but she couldn't be certain. The sound of their steps changed. They were on a gravel surface. They went down a set of stairs. Through a doorway, there was a third figure. Jenny was placed on the floor and the two figures carrying her searched her before leaving. The door was shut and the room went into almost darkness, the only light coming from a vent high up in the wall. Jenny struggled against the rope tying her. Eventually she managed to get a hand free. She removed the restraints and walked around the room. It was some sort of basement, with several areas split by stone arches. She decided not to scream and shout. It wasn't as if it would do any good.

She had no idea how long she had been in there when a hatch on the door was opened and a metal tin offered. She went over and greedily ate the contents. It smelt and tasted like chicken and potatoes but the light wasn't good enough to tell if that is what it was. As soon as the tin was empty, it was taken away. Jenny tried to find a way out but was getting angrier with herself. By the time the light from the vent faded, she had paced every square inch twice. The place was escape-proof. She gave up and settled down into a corner. Eventually, she manged to sleep. She woke to the sound of the hatch opening again. The tin was thrust through and she ate the contents. Some sort of cold porridge. Again, once it was empty, it was removed. Left with her thoughts, she tried to figure out what she knew, where she was and who these people were. The woodland had been the same side of the road as the wall which she had seen. Were the disused gates a cover, so that it looked less appealing? What was the building? Who were the silent people? She had a lot more questions than answers. The hatch opened again.

"Who are you and why were you sitting outside our haven?" A female voice asked.

"My name is Jenny and I was away from my village looking for some friends who hadn't come back on time." Jenny replied

"Where is your village?"

"West of Eastbourne." Jenny replied, staying vague.

"How many people live in your village?"

"Eighty or so. We all found each other after the virus."

"What were your friends looking for?"

"Resources, survivors, other groups. Who are you and why have you taken me?"

"I am Helene. We are a mostly peaceful group of people who wanted to live away from society before the virus. There are about thirty of us."

"Why kidnap me then?"

"We had some problems after the virus. Some people found us, tried stealing from us, killed three of our community. Now we avoid everyone. Hector and Joanne saw you while searching for wild mushrooms.

They panicked and thought taking you was the best idea."

"You could let me go." Jenny offered. "I won't mention this place to anyone."

Jenny knew it was a cliché, knew that it wouldn't work but she had nothing else to lose.

"I'm afraid that can't happen. Now you know about us we have to hold a meeting of the community to decide what to do about you. You know about us; you are a risk to us now."

"What are my options?"

"Death, stay locked up or join us. A vote will decide your fate."

The hatch closed and Jenny was once again left with her now darker and more desperate thoughts.

Chapter 49

Leo grabbed some sleep whilst Jake watched the building. He had counted at least thirty people coming and going from the building. When Leo was awake, Jake had given him an update. Leo watched as the people moved around freely. There were no weapons in sight. They all came out of the building, went the opposite way and disappeared from view before coming back into view and going back into the building. One person came out, seeming to limp slightly, and turned towards where they had seen the person with the tin the day before go. They disappeared down the stairs and after five minutes reappeared. Jake had seen it too.

"I'd like to know what is down there." Jake said

"Or who." Leo answered.

They both stayed silent, both thinking then Leo spoke first.

"I'll go. They don't appear to be watching this side. I can sneak in, take a look and sneak back."

"I was thinking the same thing. I also think it's best that you go." Jake agreed. "I'm the better shot. I can cover you from here if I need to."

Leo nodded and crawled from under the tree. He left his rucksack in place and moved with just his rifle. He stayed inside the treeline and used it to flank the lake as far as he could. He then crossed the lake using a bridge and was forced to move between trees along fairly exposed track approaching the building. He was within one hundred metres of the house when he stopped tight against a tree. Someone was walking around the side of the building, thankfully with their head down and not looking for anyone. Leo watched him as he carried

on walking and disappeared from view around the rear

of the building. Taking a cautious approach, Leo reached

the steps and went down them carefully. He found a

hatch and opened it. He looked around and was startled

but delighted to see Jenny. She was against a wall, sitting

with her head down.

#

Chapter 50

Jenny didn't look up when the hatch opened. She
didn't want to talk to Helene or anyone else. If they were
going to kill her then she wasn't going to give them the
satisfaction of begging.

"Is this the part where the hero says something
clichéd?" Leo asked.

Jenny's head snapped up at the sound of Leo's
voice. Was she dreaming? A hallucination? She looked
at the hatch and saw Leo's grinning face. How had he
found her?

"I don't have any way of unlocking the door.
Jake is on overwatch. Now I know you are here we will
get you out. Take this, keep it hidden," Leo said passing

a knife through the hatch. "If you need it, then don't hesitate. See you soon."

The hatch closed and she was alone again, full of hope. She put the knife in her pocket. She wasn't safe yet but she knew that she had a chance now. Leo had pulled off the impossible and found her. She looked around the area again, to see if there was anything else that could be used as a weapon. There was nothing, it was as if the room had been cleared especially for use as a cell. She knew Jake could pick locks, Leo would go and swap with Jake. How long that would take, she didn't know. Without a watch, she could only judge time by the light coming through the vent and where it landed on the wall. The hatch opened again.

"We will be voting this evening, If you tell us what we want to know, it will help with the verdict." Helene said.

"I'm not going to give you anything that will help you hurt my friends."

"We only want to know where they are and what resources they have. You can tell us that, surely? We aren't going to hurt them. We want to avoid them." Helene countered.

"I'm not saying anything. You can kill me before I help you." The knowledge that Jake and Leo were out there made her sound confident.

The hatch slammed shut and she was left alone again. She watched the light from the vent move across the wall. The sound of her breathing was the loudest thing she could hear. There was a scrape of metal, the door opened and a person was pushed in to join her.

#

Chapter 51

Jake watched Leo reappear and move away from the house. He disappeared from view and Jake continued looking for patterns of movement. He saw someone go down the steps and come back a minute later. He could tell by the body language that the person was angry. Leo appeared and took up a position next to him.

"Jenny is alive. She has my knife." Leo began, "I've said that you'll go back for her. I'll cover you, so you go, unlock the door and bring her back."

"I'd like to wait until it gets dark but I understand the need to get out of here." Jake agreed. "If anything goes wrong, withdraw and get help. No heroics."

Jake checked that he had everything he needed and then moved off. Following a similar route to Leo, he moved more slowly and paused more often. He reached

the track and stopped, then moved along the path using

trees as cover. He got to the last tree before the open

space and the stairs, paused and looked around. He

shifted his rifle to his back and started to cross. Without

warning a person came round the corner from the side of

the building which Leo couldn't see. The person had

their head down and wasn't paying attention. Jake

moved fast, covered the ground between them and

delivered a solid punch to the side of the person's head.

The person dropped to the floor. Jake dragged the person

down the stairs and made very short work of the padlock

on the door. As he finished, the person started to come

round. Jake grabbed the person and opened the door. He

thrust the person in and looked at Jenny.

"Let's get out of here." Jake said quickly.

Jenny nodded and headed past Jake and out of the door. Jake closed the door and relocked it. They moved fast, and soon reached the treeline where they paused. Jake checked that they weren't being followed and then led the way back to Leo. He watched as Jenny and Leo hugged each other tightly and kissed.

"I hate to be that guy but we need to get going." Jake said, breaking up the moment.

Leo and Jake grabbed their rucksacks and put them on. Jenny suddenly gasped and went pale. A look of shock and fear on her face.

#

Chapter 52

Seeing Jake and Leo put their rucksacks on had given Jenny a sudden realisation, something she had overlooked.

"They have my stuff, my map. I had drawn my route on it. They know where the village is." Jenny said.

Jake and Leo turned to look at her. The silence in the moment of realisation was awful. How had she missed that? Why hadn't she used the map without drawing her route? Had she just made things a lot worse?

"Ok, did they tell you anything about themselves?" Jake asked.

"Just that they were a group who had distanced themselves from society before the virus and that they had been attacked after the virus." Jenny said, "Why?"

"I haven't seen any weapons, they haven't harmed you, yet." Jake began, "Another group we found mentioned a group out this way but had never met them."

"You think they could be peaceful?" Leo asked, "It's a hell of a conclusion to jump to."

"I think we could try and make contact, get your stuff back." Jake stated.

Thirty minutes later and with Jenny and Leo in positions to cover him if needed Jake stepped out of the treeline and walked towards the main entrance of the house, arms stretched out either side of him and with no weapons. Someone saw him and shouted an alert. Jake stopped. He waited. A woman came out of the entrance holding a rifle. Jake stayed standing still.

"Who are you?" She shouted.

"Jake, I believe you were holding a friend of mine."

"What do you want?"

"To talk." Jake shouted.

He studied the woman, who was dressed in cargo trousers and a windproof jacket. She had a serious look on her face. The rifle was something that Jake wasn't worried about. It was a bolt action air rifle. He doubted it had the power to reach the one hundred or so metres between them.

"Talk about what?"

"Peace," Jake answered. "I suggest you check the prisoner you have. I'll wait."

The woman gave an instruction and the person who raised the alarm ran off. He came back three minutes later and reported to the woman.

"My name is Helene. Where is the girl who was in the undercroft?"

"I have released her. She is now covering me, as is one other from my group. If I give the word they will open fire. I don't know about you but I've seen enough death for many lifetimes, If Jenny can have her bag back, we shall leave and not come back, or we can look to establish links, support, trading."

"She can have her bag, What can you offer us?"

"Mutual support .We have a doctor. We have food, water, medicine, clothes, tools and more."

Jake watched as the same person went away again and came back with Jenny's rucksack. He approached and dropped the rucksack in front of Jake.

"Return one week from now We will have an answer for you then." Helene said, "Thank you for not killing anyone here today."

\#

Epilogue

Jake sat on the sofa in the living room of their house, Laura by his side, while Alex and Chloe were playing with Timber. The weather was still brutally cold. The days were short and the weather miserable. After Helene had returned Jenny's rucksack, Jake, Leo and Jenny had left, returned to the bikes and waited for Chris, Marcus and support to reach them. As soon as they saw them in the distance they had walked to them and met them. They explained what had happened and then continued heading back to Alfriston.

They had used the bikes more often, returned to Crowhurst, set up links with Jeff and Clara, and there was now a regular meet up planned for Little Common on the first Sunday of every month, at first just to catch up but trades had been discussed. Clara had visited Alfriston once. Jake had taken a group back to Helene and discussed helping each other. Helene had admitted that they had no real weapons and training in defence. Jake had offered to help fix that. Helene had accepted the offer and in the time since then Jamal had gone three times and taught basic weapon skills and shooting to some of Helene's people.

Chris had led a group to Burwash and found a group of survivors around a farm just south of the village. They had agreed to keep in touch and share information. Jake had taken a group that included Eliza and Katy up to Standen but had found it empty when they arrived. Returning to Alfriston afterwards, Jake had decided to stay back and spend more time with Laura, Alex, Chloe and Timber. Leo and Jenny had moved in together, for as

Jenny put it, 'the new normal' had replaced the old rules; before the virus an eighteen and a sixteen year old living alone together would have been unheard of. They were officially a couple and weren't hiding the fact. Will had managed to get everything they needed to plant for next year and was now working on barns and stables for the animals.

"Right, kids, are you ready to see a show?" Jake asked them.

"Yeah!" Alex and Chloe replied.

Laura made them put their coats on and all five of them including Timber stepped out into the cold evening air. They walked through the village, other residents joining them in the walk. The approached the community centre. Alex and Chloe stopped when they saw the building. It had been decorated with Christmas decorations and the solar panels had just enough charge to make the fairylights twinkle. From inside the building came the sounds of laughter and glasses clinking.

"It's our first annual Christmas Carol concert. We have even arranged for Father Christmas to visit. It turns out he survived the virus." Jake said with a subtle emphasis on the 'Chris' part of Christmas.

The End.

Printed in Great Britain
by Amazon

34363088R00126